Death Line

M. L. Hardy

I0520204

Published by: M. L. Hardy

*Library of Congress Copyright Office–COPUBS
101 Independence Avenue SE Washington, DC
20559*

"Love truth, and pardon error," Voltaire, 1738.

Prologue

This is a story of religion and death. This book is based on a true story of lives being destroyed and lost by a health care system ran by the Catholic Church.

There are many families out there who do not know their loved ones lives were cut short and covered up by the local hospital, that is centered around love, peace and forgiveness.

Ch.1

Taylor Bradford awoke on a tiring Monday morning after a night of terrible dreams. Taylor has always had dreams that seemed so real, she had to question if they were in fact real when she was awake. Last night's dream was no different. Taylor dreamt she was walking down an aisle at a funeral home, up to a pristine white casket. Black roses surrounded the casket with the petals falling slowly to the floor. The contrast between the white casket and black roses was almost blinding. When Taylor looked into the casket, lying in the soft white satin pillow was her Grandfather, Samuel Morgan. Taylor felt confusion come over her; she knew he was not dead. She thought this must be a mistake. I do not remember him dying. Surely, she would have known if he had died. She looked up from the casket and saw her grandfather's sprit dancing above the casket. Then his spirit went up in bright red flames. Then she woke up.

Ch.2

The phone call Taylor received that morning was one she did not expect. It was her Grandfather explaining he was going to stay in the hospital for some tests.

"Are you sure you are ok?" Taylor asked.
"Yes dear. I went to see my doctor about the shortness of breath I have been having and he wants to keep me here for a couple of days. Now don't worry, I will be fine. I just need you to check on your Grandmother. Your mother is going to stay with her while I am up here."
"Ok, Grandpa. Do you need anything?"
"No, your mother and Grandmother are bringing me up a few things, books, magazines, clothes, post its, and pens."
"I will come up as soon as I can." Taylor reassured her Grandfather.

Taylor hung up the phone and took a deep breath. The local hospital was a 45-minute car ride, and she worked another 45-minute drive, in the opposite direction. Taylor did not know what was to become of her Grandfather. She thought about the dream she had the previous night.

Samuel Morgan was a retired inventor, ex-Marine and now an avid fisherman. He was a very loving and meticulous man. Everything had its place and everything he did was on a list he wrote on post it notes.

Ch.3

It took Taylor a week of phone calls to the hospital and to her mother, Olivia Kingsley, to realize she needed to go see her Grandfather. Taylor drove the 45 minutes to get to St. Anthony's in Sunnyville, KS from the town she lived in Capespring. The drive was not terrible, but it did give her time to think about what had happened over the last week. Samuel had tests ran on his lungs and then biopsy's of his lungs and was found to have Chronic Obstructive Pulmonary Disease or COPD for short. Samuel's pulmonologist, Dr. Killsmen, told him he would have 5 years to get his life in order and put the final touches on his life.

When Taylor heard 5 years, she thought 5 years to a 72 year old who went into the hospital for shortness of breath, seemed to be unreasonable. Taylor approached the door to the room her Grandfather was in; she took a long deep breath before entering the room.

When she saw him, it was the same man that took her fishing, swimming and yelled at her whenever she did something that was not to his liking. She was not ready to say goodbye in 5 years. She felt like a child still when she was in his presence and thought how awful it would be to never feel like a child again.

"Hi Grandpa, how are you feeling?"

"I am tired, but they say is normal after being cut opened and having pieces of your lungs taken out."

"Yes, that does seem to be expected. How are they treating you?"

"They really don't like me writing everything down on my post its. And they are a little scary."

Taylor knew that she had a look of confusion on her face that her Grandfather picked up on immediately. "Scary?" Taylor asked.

"I am going to tell you what happened a few nights ago, but don't tell your mother and Grandmother, they will worry." Taylor nodded as Samuel continued, "I was in my room recovering from the procedure and there was a man in that bed over there with a drain tube coming out of his belly," Samuel pointed over to the empty bed next to his. "So, I assumed he had surgery like me. It was late the TV and the lights above the beds were on; I was dozing in and out. The man in the bed over there woke me up." Samuel pointed to the empty bed again next to his, "When I was dozing, he asked me to hit my call button. He had been hitting his call button for a long while and no one was coming in or talking to him over the call button. So, I said sure without even thinking. I asked him why he needed a nurse, after I hit the call button. Well, he pulled back his sheet and there was blood pouring out of his stomach area; not the tube. I gasped, and I knew all the blood that was in him was going to be on the floor in a matter of minutes. I hit my call button so many times; I don't know how many. Then the man lost consciousness as the blood was pouring on to the floor.

I started yelling 'help, help' and no one came. The man's face just dropped and his mouth came open and I knew he was gone. I continued to yell for help. Finally, a male nurse came in and as if I was bothering him, said 'what are you yelling about?' I looked him strait in the face and said 'he's dead.' That is not the worst part. Well, that is pretty horrible, but then the male nurse checked for a pulse and left the room. He left me there with this poor man, who died because of his ignorance. A few minutes later a whole group of nurses came in and all looked at the man and the floor that was covered in his blood. They pulled the curtain around me so I could not see what they were doing, but I heard them. They were saying things like 'What are we going to do?' 'How can we make this look like surgical complications?' 'Even if we lie, there is a witness.' I did not know what they were going to do with me or to me."

Taylor's face was a shade of pale white. She knew her grandfather was a strong man and had seen many things, being a Korean War Veteran, but to have this happen in front of you when you cannot jump out of bed and run away must have scared him.

"What did you do?" Taylor asked.

"Well nothing, I did not know what to do. Call the Police and tell them there was a murder in front of me and by the way I am in a hospital bed. I did not think anyone would believe me, but in the morning Dr. Killsmen came to see me. He asked me questions about what I saw and heard. He already knew, I could tell by the way he was questioning me. So, I told him it was a real shame about the man. I did not even know his name."

"Grandpa, are you ok with not telling anyone about this?"

"No, but I really don't want to die yet. I want those 5 years the doctors are telling me I have."

Taylor was concerned about her Grandfather's safety and for his sanity.

Ch. 4

The day came when Taylor could take her Grandfather home. It had been 3 long weeks of driving back and forth to the hospital to make sure Samuel was ok. Taylor's Grandmother, Sarah Morgan, had been great through it all. Sarah had a slight case of dementia and was forgetting little things every now and then.
Life was going to be different. Samuel had been put on oxygen and had to be in a wheel chair for walking long distances. Dr. Killsmen said Samuel's lungs needed time to recover after the surgery and it would take some time for them to go back to the way they were before he went into the hospital.

When Taylor pulled into the drive at her Grandparents house her Grandfather said.
"All this for me?"
"Well how did you think we were going to get you in the house?" Taylor replied.
Samuel Morgan was a large man 6'2 and weighing 250 pounds.

Taylor's father, Jerry Kingsley, and her husband, Kenny Bradford, built a wheel chair ramp from the driveway leading up to the house.

The 100-acre ranch was nestled in the woods away from traffic and paved roads. It was a beautiful sight to Samuel. He had built the little log cabin out of trees he cut and treated. Samuel had nights in the hospital he did not know if he would ever see his creation again, he called home.

Everyone came out to greet and help get Samuel in the house. There were many new things in the house, which had not been there before Samuel went into the hospital: a bedside commode, an oxygen regulator, many oxygen hoses strung throughout the house and many oxygen tanks in the closet.

"I am so glad to finally be home. Thank you all for your help." Samuel said to everyone. Taylor was smiling and trying not to think of the next 5 years and what was to come.
Taylor left that night happy to know her Grandfather made it home and was still alive. She thought to herself on her way home, now she could do something for that poor man who lost his life, so needlessly; if not for him maybe his family who do not know the truth.

Ch.5

The next few days went by so fast. Taylor would go to work, come home and, she and Kenny would drive to her Grandparents to check on her Grandfather. Taylor's Mother, Olivia, had been staying at the ranch to help with the animals, at least that is what she told Samuel. Taylor received daily reports on his health from her mother and his progress, mentally.

Samuel seemed to be adjusting to his new lifestyle of having to be wheeled outside and always having his oxygen on. Samuel was even inventing a trailer that he could have towed behind his truck and put directly into the lake, so he could fish from his wheel chair. Yes, it seemed to be all going well and Taylor was going to enjoy and soak up every second of the next 5 years.

Ch.6

The telephone rang at Taylor's house at 5:30am on the following Sunday, Samuel had been home one week.

"Taylor!" Olivia screamed into the phone.
"Mom is that you?"
"It's Grandpa, he turned blue and his blood pressure dropped and I can't find a pulse."
"Did you call 911?"
"Yes, the fire department and the ambulance are on the way."
Taylor knew she was closer to her Grandparents house than the ambulance or the fire department. "I am on my way."

Taylor leapt from her bed and told Kenny what was happening.
"I will drive you," Kenny said.

When they arrived at the end of the lane Taylor's father was waiting there for the ambulance to direct them to the ranch.
"A volunteer fireman lived only a few miles away and came strait here and he is already there with your Grandfather," said Jerry.

Taylor left Kenny with her father and floored her SUV down the bumpy lane that only a week ago she brought her Grandfather home in.

Ch.7

The next few minutes were in slow motion and did not seem real to Taylor. There was a man doing CPR on her Grandfather while her Mother and Grandmother watched. The fireman called for Life Line, which is the helicopter used to transport people who would not make it the 45-minute drive to the hospital, alive.

Taylor took her mother and Grandmother outside when the ambulance arrived at the ranch to wait on the helicopter. When she saw the white, massive, loud helicopter fly over the hills and trees and land on the ranch, it seemed unbelievable to Taylor. Uncertainty filled Taylor, she did not know if he was alive or dead, but she did know she did not want him to die in that metal contraption; leaving his whole life and everything he loved below.

When they brought Samuel out of the log cabin he was pale and unconscious. Samuel had been intubated with an ambubag attached to his mouth, which one of the flight nurses was squeezing over and over. As the helicopter took off, Taylor thought that would be the last time she saw her Grandfather.

"They are taking him to St. Anthony's," one of the firemen said, to Taylor as the Life Line took flight.

"St. Anthony's?" Taylor said very quietly under her breath. If Samuel did make it to the hospital would he make it out of St. Anthony's a second time, Taylor wondered? St. Anthony's was the last place Taylor wanted her Grandfather to go to, but it was the only hospital for another 60 miles past St. Anthony's. Taylor told her mother and Grandmother to follow behind her up to the hospital.

Kenny and her father stayed behind to take care of the farm.

The drive to the hospital was one Taylor hopped she would never have to make. Taylor wanted her Grandfather to die in his home, his creation, he was so proud of. She did not want him to die in route to a hospital aboard Life Line. Not just any hospital, but the very hospital that scared Samuel Morgan to the core.

As she drove, Taylor thought about the previous summer with her Grandfather, working on her and Kenny's new, but used boat. Taylor had never owned a boat, but grew up on her Grandparents many boats. Her Grandfather always had a couple of boats that he worked on and one that he used when he went fishing. Taylor always loved being out on the water and just sitting in the boat relaxing, while her Grandfather fished. Taylor was not much of a fisherman, but always did her part in catching a few keepers. Taylor thought back to her Grandfather telling her how to recover the seats on the old boat and how to change out the fuel tanks. The first time Kenny and Taylor took their boat out for its maiden voyage, Samuel was right there, telling her how to back a trailer into the water and how to back the boat out of the trailer. He never lost his temper, but would sternly tell them both how to do things the right way on the water. "Make sure you stay to the deep side of the channel, don't get too close to the shore; you are going to hit a sandbar if you continue to drive like that," Taylor could hear his voice in her mind.

Ch.8

The waiting room in the ICU unit at St. Anthony's was crammed with people and there were pillows and blankets strung everywhere. People where watching TV, reading, and talking on the phone.

Taylor wanted to know what was going on with her Grandfather. The kind nun at the admission desk told Taylor and her family to go to the ICU waiting room and someone would talk to them shortly. Over an hour had passed and no one had entered the waiting room that was a medical professional. Taylor was not one to wait. There was a clear sign on the door it said 'Do Not Enter.' Taylor did not listen to authority all the time, so she walked through the doors and entered a totally different world. There were alarms sounding and people talking and nurses and doctors running all over the small area. Taylor walked up to the large desk, which was centered in the middle of a small area. Surrounding the desk were 7 small rooms with glass sliding doors. Taylor approached the first person she saw behind the desk.

"Hi, I need to see how Samuel Morgan is doing?" Taylor said to a nurse behind the desk. "And you are?" said the nurse who was not in a particularly good mood. A large scowl shown all over the nurse's face.

"I am his Granddaughter. My family and I have been waiting over an hour to find out how he is. He was brought by helicopter."

"No one has come and talked to you?"

"Nope," Taylor said smartly.

At that time Taylor's mother and Grandmother came through the same door Taylor did.

"Well if you would follow me I will take you to him," said the nurse.

Taylor entered one of the small rooms behind the nurse. There were numerous machines blinking and making beeping sounds. Lying in the middle of them was her Grandfather. He was alive. The machine breathing for him was the loudest and Samuel was not moving, but merely lying silently, with his chest rising and falling with the sound of the machine. Sarah ran to Samuel's side and Taylor and her mother just stood there in awe.

"Is he going to be ok?" Taylor asked the nurse, all the while keeping her eyes on Samuel.

"I am going to let his doctor come and talk to you," replied the nurse.

Ch. 9

The 10-minute wait for the doctor seemed like hours to Taylor. The only thing she could do is watch as her Grandfather's chest rose and fell with the ventilator.

"Hello, I am Dr. Martin. I am Samuel's Internal Medicine Doctor and I am heading up his care with a group of specialists."

Olivia shook his hand and introduced Taylor and her Grandmother. "It is finally nice to meet you," Olivia said.

"Yes, I do believe I have talked to you and your daughter on the phone a few times. Well, Samuel is in critical condition. His lungs have stopped working properly and caused him to have several M.I.'s or heart attacks. Right now, the ventilator is breathing for him, so oxygen can get to his blood and vital organs."

"Was there damage to his heart?" Asked Olivia. "Yes, we are not sure to what extent as of yet, but will we will know more tomorrow. There is a cardiologist, a urologist and of course a pulmonologist working on his care."

"A urologist?" asked Taylor.

"Yes, Samuel is in kidney failure caused from the lack of oxygen his lungs were providing his vital organs," stated Dr. Martin.

"What are his chances?" asked Olivia.

"None," stated Sarah. She was still standing next to Samuel holding his hand.

"Well, I am not saying we are going to run some tests and we will know more tomorrow. He is not going to wake up tonight, we are keeping him heavily sedated," said Dr. Martin.

Tears were falling from Taylor's eyes as the doctor kept speaking. She did not wipe them away. "What happened to the 5 years he was given, I don't remember anyone saying 7 days." Taylor said angrily.

"I suggest you all go home tonight and get some rest and we will know more tomorrow afternoon," suggested Dr. Martin.

"Can we stay a little while?" asked Sarah still not leaving Samuel's side.

"Yes, but visiting hours are up and the ICU has strict rules, so take a few minutes and then tomorrow you can see him at 9am again," said Dr. Martin.

"Ok, but do you have his advance directive?" Olivia asked.

"Yes, I have a copy, but if you would bring the original tomorrow, I would appreciate it." Dr. Martin said.

"Yes, of course," said Olivia.

"Good night and see you tomorrow," Dr. Martin said as he waved goodbye and left the little glass room.

"Advance directive?" questioned Taylor.

"Yes, your grandparents drew these up with their Will. They wanted to make sure they were not kept alive by machines or tubes if it ever came to it." Taylor's mother said.

"Who is supposed to unplug them?" Taylor said hastily.

"Me," said Olivia with a tear running down her cheek.

Ch.10

The three women left the hospital that night and went home. Taylor was numb by the time she got home. Kenny was waiting up for her and she told him everything she knew, but it did not seem like much. Taylor's mother said she would go to the hospital the next day and Taylor should go to work and she would call her to tell her what the doctors said.

Taylor did not want to go to work, but knew she could not do anything at the hospital. The next morning was a difficult Monday morning. Most Monday's were hard, but this one seemed to be the hardest Monday she had ever had. While Taylor was at work she kept busy, so she did not stop to think about her Grandfather. The telephone rang at her desk and Taylor answered on the first ring, "Hello."

"Taylor, I don't know what the doctors are trying to do? They put a feeding tube in Grandpa and are taking him in and out of the room, Olivia said.

"Did one of the doctors come and talk to you?"

"Yes, the cardiologist was here and the urologist. They are going to start him on dialysis for the kidney failure and they want to do heart surgery."

"What? They can't do all of that he is not strong enough," exclaimed Taylor. "I am going to call Dr. Killsmen and see what he thinks about all of this." Taylor knew Dr. Killsmen was a good pulmonologist and he was brutally honest.

Taylor immediately dialed the number to the hospital and asked for Dr. Killsmen to be paged. The Nun on the other line wanted to know if this was an emergency.

"Look, sister, or mother, or whatever your name is, I want to talk to him now," Taylor said sternly.

"Very well, it will be a few moments if he is even here in the hospital," said the nun.

Taylor waited on hold and then a calm quiet voice came on the line.

"This is Dr. Killsmen."

"Hi, Doctor I am Taylor Bradford, Samuel Morgan's Granddaughter and I am calling concerning the other doctors that want to do surgery and dialysis on him.

I don't think he is strong enough."

"You are correct Ms. Bradford; Samuel will not make it through surgery. His lungs are turning to stone and will stop expanding even with the ventilator breathing for him. I told the other doctors this, but they felt that your family wanted to save him or try everything to do so. I am not in agreement. I feel your family should shut off the ventilator and let him go on his own."

"Let him go?" Taylor was standing in her office as tears started to fall from her eyes again.

"Yes, Ms. Bradford, I am sorry, but there is nothing that will save him except a lung transplant, but he is too old and his heart could not take that. If I were you I would tell your mother to sign the order to shut off the ventilator."

"I want you to wake my Grandfather up before shutting it off."

"We normally don't do that, Ms. Bradford, it is better if they just sleep through it all."

"No, I want to talk to him and say goodbye," Taylor said without sobbing.

"It will take a little while but ok I will give the order to stop the meds and let him wake up. He will be in pain, so I want him to have some morphine, to ease the pain," said Dr. Killsmen in a stern, but still quiet voice. "His lungs will have to work overtime to compensate, since the ventilator will be off."

"Ok, I will talk to my mother and grandmother. Don't shut it off until we are all there." Taylor said like she was giving a direct order.

"Yes, Ms. Bradford. Goodbye and I will talk to you soon."

"Goodbye Doctor."

Taylor hung up the phone and started sobbing. Taylor was trying to get up the courage to call her mother back. She did not know how her mother would take the news of her father dying and having to sign the order that would allow him to die.

Taylor took a deep breath, wiped her tears and dialed.

"Mom, I talked to Dr. Killsmen and he thinks we should shut off the ventilator and let Grandpa go."

"Are you sure that is what he said?" Olivia asked as she started to cry.

Taylor was now sobbing again. "Yes, I am sure. I am leaving now and I will be there in about an hour and half. Dr. Killsmen is going to let us wake him up before shutting off the ventilator."

"No more medicine?"

"No more medicine mom, there is nothing the medicine can do for him," said Taylor now trying to control her emotions.

Ch.11

Taylor drove the 90 miles from her work to the hospital, while making phone calls. First she called Kenny who was working. She told him to call her sister, Dawn Kingsley, in Alabama and tell her what was going on. Taylor knew her sister would want to say good-bye to their Grandfather. Dawn was living in Alabama with her boyfriend and had not been able to come home, due to money problems and the high cost of flying. Taylor was sure now her mother and father would pay for her to come home at least for the funeral.

Taylor was feeling the immense pressure of what was to come in the next few days. She was not sure of the procedure of letting someone just go off the ventilator, but knew it would be hard to say goodbye to the man who had shown her many things in life. He was always the first to say what he felt and never held back. Taylor was still thinking about the dream she had only few short weeks ago. She had brushed it off as a nightmare. Could it be she was to try and save the soul of the one man who never set foot in a church except for funerals, weddings, or the rare occasion she begged him to go on holidays? Taylor was a youth pastor and a Christian. She was not a "bible thumper," but a good person who always taught the children in her church to do good and love Jesus. Taylor was the only person in her family who went to church every Sunday. She felt she was the connection to god for her entire family. Her family was all Christians, but they never attended church regularly and never prayed or gave their life up to god. Even Kenny was a Christian, but only went to church when he was forced and even then was not happy about it. Kenny thought church is anywhere you wanted it to be.

Taylor prayed for Samuel while she was driving. "Dear God, if it is your will for him to go, please let it be peaceful. I want him to be received unto you, I ask of you to accept him for who he is and what he has done. Dear Lord, please hear my prayer," Taylor said aloud in the car as she drove.

Ch.12

Taylor walked up to the ICU and was met by that all too familiar sign, 'Do Not Enter' and below were the pathetic visiting hours the hospital staff thought would be less inconvenient for them. Taylor walked through the double doors knowing everyone was sitting in the waiting room wanted to do the same thing. Some people would wait hours for 30 minutes with their loved ones.

Taylor walked past the nurses' station and directly into her Grandfather's room. There she saw Dr. Killsmen, her mother, and grandmother standing around Samuel.

"He is starting to wake up," exclaimed Olivia.

"Already?" questioned Taylor.

"Yes, he has not received any sedation in quite a few hours, so he should be able to talk to me," said Dr. Killsmen. He walked over to Samuel's bedside and placed his hand on Samuel's shoulder and leaned in close. "Samuel, do you know who I am?" asked the Doctor.

Samuel nodded his head up and down.

"Your family is here, and they wanted me to wake you up before taking the tube out of your throat. I am going to tell you what will happen, ok?"

Once again Samuel's head nodded yes.

"If I stop this machine from breathing for you and take this tube out you will eventually stop breathing and die. I want you to know I have talked to your family and they agree you would not want to be hooked up to a ventilator to extend your life."

Samuel nodded in agreement.

Taylor was welling up inside and did not know how long she could hold all of her tears in.

"I am going to give you a few minutes with your family while I go get the respiratory therapist to help me unintubate you."

Samuel nodded as a tear fell from his cheek. Sarah was now holding his hand and crying with him.

"Hi, Grandpa," said Taylor.

"Hi, Dad," said Olivia standing behind Taylor.

"I love you and want you to know everything will be ok," said Taylor in a reassured voice, taking his hand in hers.

Samuel looked directly into Taylor's eyes and just stared.

Taylor was not sure he agreed with her, when she said everything would be ok, but was sure he understood her. Taylor felt a shiver go over her entire body. The coldness started at her hands, and then traveled to her entire body in just a split second.

The therapist and doctor came in together and asked the family to go on the other side of the curtain and wait until they were done.

Taylor, Olivia and Sarah just stood there not knowing what was to come. Would he die in a matter of minutes or hours or would it be days? Taylor heard the doctor tell Samuel to cough loudly when he said to and then the tube would be out of his throat.

"Cough now," said the doctor.

Samuel let out the loudest, most horrible, cough Taylor had ever heard followed by gagging sounds.

The curtain opened and the therapist was fixing Samuel's pillow and setting him up in bed. "He will be able to whisper, but not talk for a while," said Dr. Killsmen.

"How long will he live?" asked Olivia.

"It is hard to tell, he is a large and strong man so a few hours to a few days. I want you all to know this will be a horrible death, not pretty, by any means," said Dr. Killsmen.

"Death is never pretty, I assure you," said Sarah as she walked back into the room.

"I want you to be prepared for the worst," assured Dr. Killsmen.

"We are," said Olivia.

"I will be back later to check on him, if you need anything tell Angela, she is the nurse that will be taking care of him tonight," he said as he walked down the hall to the nurses' station.

Taylor walked into the room and saw Samuel sitting upright in his bed and he was smiling at her.

"Has he said anything yet?" Taylor asked the therapist and her Grandmother.

"No," said the therapist, as she walked out of the room.

Samuel was pale and he was perspiring. He was perspiring so much, his pillow was beginning to show saturation of sweat behind his head.

Taylor walked up to him and held his hand and said, "How do you feel?" His hand was hot and wet to Taylor. She looked into his eyes.

"6,6,6" Samuel whispered.

"What?" Taylor asked as if she did not hear him correctly. Olivia was on the other side of the bed with her ear to his chest and Sarah had taken a seat in one of the chairs in the small room.

"6,6,6," whispered Samuel again to Taylor.

"I don't understand what you mean by 6,6,6?" Taylor said in quiet voice so Sarah would not hear her.

Olivia was looking shocked as well as confused by what she heard.

Then Samuel gave Taylor the scariest look she had ever seen him make. His face was not the kind, gentle, and loving Grandfather she had always known, but that of a stranger who was giving her, the evilest look. Taylor looked at her mother and then back down at Samuel who was staring into her face intently.

One last time before Taylor backed away; she put her ear to his lips and whispered, "What are you talking about?"

Samuel's lips pushed out a dry hot, "6,6,6."

The nurse entered into the room with ice chips and water and told them to offer them to Samuel and get him to take as many as he could. Olivia took the ice chips from the nurse and started to put them in his mouth. Whether it was to keep him quiet or to clean his mouth out Taylor did not know.

Ch.13

Samuel drifted in and out of sleep for the next few hours and his breathing had become labored and he was spiking temperatures up to 103. Taylor was not sure why he would have a temperature, so high after taking all the meds and the ventilator away. The nurses would come in once every hour to take Samuel's vitals and to see if the family needed anything.

"I am going to call Kenny and get something to drink," Taylor told her mother who was sitting in a chair next to Sarah in the small room.

It was now 12:00 am and the hospital was quiet and everyone was sleeping in their beds. Taylor walked out into the waiting room where more people were sleeping on cots and on the floor. Taylor kept walking and went down a set of elevators to the Emergency room exit, which was the only one open at that time of night. The cool crisp breeze fell on her face and felt wonderful. The fresh air she had not breathed since late afternoon was welcoming. Taylor got out her cell phone and dialed Kenny at home.

"Hi," said Kenny.

"Hi, I just wanted to let you know that we are still here at the hospital and Grandpa is not doing so well," replied Taylor.

"Ok, do they know how long it is going to be?" asked Kenny.

"No, the doctor said it could take hours or even days for him to stop breathing. I feel like I am sitting in that small room waiting for a miracle to happen."

"I don't know if that is going to happen, honey, but your sister will be here tomorrow. Your Dad is paying for her plane ticket and I am going to pick her up at the airport," said Kenny.

"Great, I can't wait to see her. I know my mom will be happy too," said Taylor.

"Try to rest tonight and I will see you in the afternoon after I go to the airport," said Kenny.

"I don't know how much rest I will get, but I will try. I Love you,"

"Love you too, bye,"

"Bye," Taylor replied as she wished she was in bed lying next to him. Taylor hung up her phone and took a deep breath of fresh air and walked back into the hospital. The air inside the hospital was heavy and was saddening to her. As she walked up to pop machine she started putting money in it. Taylor looked down the long hallway and saw a man walking towards her. His face was indiscernible to her, he was tall and wearing all black. As he strode closer Taylor saw the white in the middle of his neckline.

"Father," said Taylor in a quiet voice as the man strode past.

"Hello, how are you this evening?" asked the man as he paused in front of her.

"As good as can be expected I suppose," replied Taylor.

"If you need anything Mrs. Bradford just let me know," said the priest as he turned to walk away.

"How did you know my name?" Taylor asked as the priest continued to walk down the hallway. She did not get a response, but a mere hand waving as he continued to walk away.

Taylor turned back to the pop machine and finished putting the money in and got her drink and walked to the elevators to go back up to Samuel's room.

Taylor got off the elevators and walked down to the ICU and the door to the Doctors lounge was open and Taylor peered in. The room was well lit and the tables were large with dozens of black chairs around the tables. Each table had a centerpiece. The centerpiece was a tray with drinks and cups. There were a few doctors sitting there in the room and they were talking about patients and what the next step would be for caring for them. Taylor heard a familiar voice; Dr. Martin was in the room and another Doctor. They were quietly talking. When Taylor heard her grandfather's name her ears were tuning in and she was getting an increased sense of hearing. It was like a clearing in her hearing and she could hear everything they were saying. "Mr. Morgan should be gone by the end of the night. His vitals are not stable and his temperature is rising. I just wish we could have gotten a chance to do the surgeries, before they decided to shut of the vent. It would have been a few hundred thousand dollars we could have billed for," said the doctor Taylor did not know.

"Yes, that would have been nice, but Dr. Killsmen keeps butting in and trying to help these families make these decisions about life and death before we can run up these hospital bills and Mr. Morgan has great insurance; plus he has a secondary insurance, that would have been a nice bonus," said Dr. Morgan. "Oh, well there will always be more patients with private insurance needing expensive testing and procedures."

"Yes, there sure will," said the other Doctor, in a reassuring voice.

Taylor crept back into the hallway and knew neither of the doctors saw her. Taylor had always thought doctors did things were in the patients' best interest, not their wallet's best interest.

Taylor walked back into the room and Sarah had fallen asleep and Olivia was standing over Samuel's bed and he was smiling at her.

"You're awake?" asked Taylor.

"Yes, I am," whispered Samuel.

"I am going to go to the restroom and take Mom for a walk, we will be back," said Olivia.

Taylor walked up to Samuel's bedside and sat down.

"I want you to know this was a hard decision for mom to make," said Taylor.

"I know," replied Samuel as he struggled to take in a deep breath.

"I also want to tell you I am going to miss you," Taylor began to cry as she said this.

"I mean really, really miss you."

Samuel gave a saddened smile and grabbed her hand and held it tightly.

Taylor stood up and gave him a kiss on the cheek and sat back down in the chair.

"I want you to look after your mother and grandmother," Samuel said still holding Taylor's hand.

"I will try, but you do such a good job of looking after all of us, I can't do it as well as you."

"Just try," replied Samuel.

Olivia and Sarah came back in the room and they all stood around Samuel and held hands and tried to smile as tears fell on to Samuel and his bed.

"Well I am ready," said Samuel looking up at the women standing over his bed.

"Ready for what? Do you think you are going somewhere?" asked Taylor.

"I am ready to go now," said Samuel.

"I don't think it works quite like that," said Olivia. "I will go and see if the nurse can bring you some morphine to help you get some rest dad."

"Yes, morphine, that would be good," said Samuel in an almost cheerful voice.

Taylor sat and held her Grandfathers hand as the nurse came in with her mother and put some medicine from a syringe in his arm. Samuel fell asleep within a few minutes.

Sarah fell asleep, as well, in the chair next to the bed with her head lying on Samuel's arm.

Taylor and her mother sat down on the floor and just looked at the two people before them.

"What do you think he meant by 6,6,6?" whispered Taylor, to her mother.

"I am not sure, maybe he thinks he is condemned or this situation he is in is like hell," replied Olivia.

"I don't know, but that look he gave me when I questioned him was scary."

"Taylor your grandfather was not a religious man and now he is dying and probably scared himself," said Olivia.

"Maybe. Dawn will be here tomorrow. Kenny is going to pick her up at the airport and bring her here in the afternoon," Taylor said.

"It will be good to have her here; I think I am going to take your Grandmother home to get some rest. It is nearly 2:00 in the morning. You should get some rest as well."

"Yea, I will, but I am going to stay and keep Grandpa company."

Olivia went over and woke Sarah up and they left after kissing Samuel goodbye. He did not notice in his mindless state of oblivion.

Taylor continued to sit on the floor in the room and watch Samuel's vitals. His heart rate was fluctuating from 180 to 30 beats per minute and Taylor knew it was not a good sign. The alarm on the monitor was recording his vital signs was showing bright red at the top and Taylor could not take her eyes off of it.

Ch.14

The next few hours seemed like days to Taylor.
She sat and prayed for just 1 minute of sleep to
feel like hours. Taylor would start to close her
eyes and the alarm on Samuels monitor would
flash red and it would startle her and she would
be fully alert until the red light would go off.
Taylor prayed for hours and drifted in and out
of consciousness, until Samuel began to wake
up and moan in pain. Taylor could hear his
breathing was beginning to become more
labored and more painful for him even as he
slept. Taylor sat on the floor hoping if she
prayed enough for Samuel, he would be
forgiven and sent to heaven. Taylor thought of
nothing else night. What could she do to help
him cross over into eternal life with Jesus?

Taylor thought back to the previous Christmas when she made her whole family come to church with her. It took many phone calls and begging to get her grandfather to go to church. Samuel sat in the pew next to Taylor and smiled at her that sheepish smile he always gave her. After church service she had asked him if he liked the service, and he replied, "It was not a complete waste of time." Taylor just laughed and smiled at him. Now at the hospital, Taylor hoped the little time Samuel spent in church worshiping Jesus was enough to help Samuel accept Jesus.

Taylor could not imagine spending eternity in heaven without her Grandfather there. He was a good man and had done many good things in his life, but would that be enough. Taylor had to tell herself, yes it was good enough.

The nurse came in at 4:30am to check on Samuel one more time before her shift was over.

"Hello, he is not sleeping well, is there anything we can do to make him more comfortable?" asked Taylor.

"I am going to give him a dose of Morphine and I will move him on to his other side and that might make him more comfortable. The day shift is going to come on and the nurse will only come in the room if he needs anything, we won't be taking any more vitals or checking on him. So if he needs anything come and get someone," explained the nurse.

"Are his vitals bad?" asked Taylor.

"Yes, his blood pressure has dropped and his heart rate is all over the place, so, it won't be long now," said the nurse.

"My mom and Grandmother went home to sleep and come back later this the morning should I wake them?"

"I think it will be a quiet a few hours. Let me show you something." Taylor got up off the floor and the nurse pulled up the sheet off of Samuel's feet and legs. "When the purple color on his feet starts to spread up to his legs then call your mother. This happens as the blood stops producing enough oxygen to all the limbs." Taylor looked down at her Grandfathers feet and they were turning purple. Taylor looked up at the monitor it had the red alarm on now, for quite some time. The O2 line was reading 88, 82, 86, 80. Samuel's lungs were shutting down and Taylor knew this would be the end of Samuel Morgan. He would die in a hospital bed. Not in his boat fishing as he had always told her is how he wanted to go. "And then just throw me over board and I will rest with the fish," Taylor remembered him saying.

The nurse gave Samuel another injection of Morphine in his arm and turned him with the help of other nurses.

"Thank you," said Taylor to the nurse as she left. "You're welcome and god bless you," said the nurse as she turned and smiled.

The room was darker now all the monitors had been shut off and the red light was no longer showing. Taylor knew she would have to watch and listen to Samuel closer to know if he was alive or gone. She felt like she had been made to say awake for years and she would never get to fully rest again, but she fell asleep for what seemed like hours in the chair next to the bed with her hand on Samuel's chest and her head on the bed. The sun came up and was showing brightly morning. The light was shining directly on to the hospital bed.

Taylor woke to a hand brushing her face and she looked up and saw Samuel staring down at her.

"Good morning," Taylor said.

"Good," Samuel took in a large gasp of air "morning." Then he groaned in pain and frustration. He did not want to wake up that morning. Samuel wanted to go to sleep the previous night and not wake up, just keep sleeping forever and ever. Samuel managed to smile at her and drifted back to sleep.

Taylor went out to the hallway and asked the nurse if Samuel could have more morphine due to him groaning in pain. The nurse said the doctor said he could have as much as was needed to ease his pain.

The nurse went into the room and Taylor looked at the clock at the nurses' station, it was 8am already. Time had flown by and yet it seemed like she had been at the hospital for days. She was wearing the same clothes she went to work in the previous day and she felt awful. Taylor did not want to call and wake up her mother and grandmother yet so she went to the restroom and called Kenny.

"Good morning, how are you on this horrible day," asked Taylor when Kenny answered the phone.

"I am ok, but you don't sound so good."

"I am mentally and physically exhausted."

"I am sorry, honey, I will be there this afternoon. I called your work and Pastor Jim was more than willing to let you have as much time off as you needed."

"Thank you. I forgot to call him last night. Are you on your way to the airport?"

"Yes, I should be there in about 30 minutes."

"Good, have Dawn call me when you get back to the car."

"I will and do you need anything?"

"A bath, change of clothes and a bed. Other than that I am good."

"I can't do any of that right now, but I will tell you I love you and missed you last night."

"I missed you too and I love you. Well I better get back to the room the nurse should be done with Grandpa."

"Alright, talk to you soon."

"Bye."

Taylor thought to herself how lucky she was to find Kenny. He was always there when she needed him and even when she did not want anyone around he was there to love her. And now when she needed him the most he was there supporting her and helping her family. Taylor hung up her phone and walked back to Samuel's room. The room was fully lit by sunlight. Samuel was not breathing well and so Taylor lifted the sheet off of his feet and looked at them intently, remembering what the night nurse told her. The purple coloring had moved a lot since 4:30 this morning. Samuel's legs had started turning the light shade of purple and had a bluish tint to them. Taylor put Samuel's sheet back around his feet and tucked him in, like her mother use to do to her when she was a child. Then she walked up to the head of the bed and kissed him on the forehead and said, "It is ok to go, everything will be fine. There are a lot of people that have waited a long time to see you again, but I am going to miss you so much. I hope you know you are so loved and will be missed by Grandma, Mom, Dad, Kenny and Dawn.

We will always remember you." Taylor took in a deep breath and so did Samuel for one last time. Taylor whispered looking up towards the ceiling, "I love you." Samuel's jaw dropped open and Taylor looked back down at him and closed his mouth and held his face with her hand as tears fell on to his cheeks.

Taylor stood over Samuel's body for some time and hugged him and gave him one last kiss on the forehead with tears streaming down her face. No one came into the room because no one knew he was gone. Taylor felt if she did not say the words it might not be true. It seemed like hours had passed when Taylor's cell phone rang and made her snap back into reality. Taylor looked at the caller ID and saw it was her mother calling, so she walked over to the doorway of the small room and answered in a sad voice.
"He's gone."
"Taylor, are you ok?"
"Yes, mom, did you hear me?"
"I heard you. Your Grandmother and I will be there in a few minutes. Did you tell the nurses?"
"No, I have not left the room yet."
"Go and tell someone and we will be there in a few minutes. I love you."
"Love you to mom." Taylor sobbed.

Ch.15

Taylor hung up the cell phone and put in back into her pocket and walked out of the room and saw a nurse walking past.

"Excuse me,"

"Yes," the nurse said as she turned and saw Taylor's face. "Are you ok?"

"My Grandfather is gone; I mean he passed away a short time ago."

"Ok, I will be in, just a second; I have to go get another nurse to confirm the death with me."

Taylor turned around and went back into the room and began to pray. Psalms 23 from the bible seemed to be the first thing that came to her mind as she sat down next to Samuel's bed.

'Yea, though I walk through the valley of the shadow of death, I will fear no evil: for thou art with me' Taylor kept repeating this over and over in her mind. She did not understand why this passage came to her. Taylor knew so many bible verses and scriptures, but this one was just running over and over in her mind.

The two nurses came back into the room, the one she found in the hallway and another much younger and larger one came in, both with their stethoscopes around their necks. The first one put her stethoscope up to Samuel's chest and nodded yes. Then the second one came up and listened for a few minutes and nodded in agreement.

"I am so sorry, I will send up the father to say a few words, if it is ok with you," said the first nurse.

"Yes, but I don't want him moved until my mother gets here."

"Ok, the father will be in shortly."

Taylor wondered what the "father" would say. She was not catholic and no one in her family was catholic. Taylor was a non-denominational youth pastor and taught about Christianity and faith not Catholicism. She knew Catholic Priest's often like to do last rights, but Samuel was already gone, all that was left was his body. Taylor thought as she sat and waited for her mother, where had he gone? Did he go up in flames as she had dreamt? Taylor hopped she would see her Grandfather once again many, many years from now. Taylor was only 27 and had many things she still wished to do here on earth and she knew her Grandfather had lived a long and wonderful life for 72 years.

The door opened and in walked a man with a bible in his hand and a rosary in his other. Taylor stood up and gave a sad smile.

"I am so sorry for your loss, child," said the father. He was wearing the traditional all black with a white collar. Taylor felt very uncomfortable, but she was always polite.

"Thank you, father. My mother and Grandmother will be here any minute now, so I don't want to do anything until then."

"Yes that is fine. My name is Father Morris. I came in to see if you needed anything."

"No, I am fine, but thank you anyway."

"I will wait outside if you need anything just let me know."

"Ok, I am just going to wait here for my family."

———

56

Father Morris exited the room and Taylor was again alone with her Grandfather's body. Taylor looked down at him again and noticed he had fluid coming from his mouth and nose. Taylor did not know much about dying, but knew Samuel would not have wanted to be seen like that. Taylor walked over to the sink in the room and got a washcloth and wetted it down and washed Samuels face. Taylor looked at his face after it was washed and felt like she had just done something, something small and insignificant, but she was doing something. Taylor put the washcloth back into the sink and the door opened once again and it was her mother and grandmother.

"I am so glad you are here."

. Taylor did not know much about dying, but knew Samuel would not have wanted to be seen like that. Taylor walked over to the sink in the room and got a washcloth and wetted it down and washed Samuels face. Taylor looked at his face after it was washed and felt like she had just done something, something small and insignificant, but she was doing something. Taylor put the washcloth back into the sink and the door opened once again and it was her mother and grandmother.

"I am so glad you are here."

"Let's give Grandma a few moments, Taylor." Said Olivia

Taylor nodded and gave her Grandmother a hug and walked out of the room with her mother.

"Mom, this is Father Morris."

Olivia shook the Father's hand.

"I am here for anything your family needs. We will take care of all the preparations if you would like."

"No, that won't be necessary. My husband is contacting the funeral home we will be using."

"Mom, can we use my church for the funeral?"

"Yes, Taylor that would be fine."

"How about I come in and say a few words then?" asked Father Morris.

"That would be ok," replied Olivia.

All three reentered the room as Sarah was holding Samuel's hand and crying. Olivia went to her and put her arms around her to console her. Taylor walked over and stood on the other side of the bed and Father Morris stood next to her.

"We are going to say a prayer now. Dear Heavenly Father please be with this family in their time of need. And now to quote a scripture." Taylor looked up and Father Morris was opening his bible to a marked page and he began " *'The Lord is my Shepherd; I shall not want. He maketh me to lie down in green pastures: he leadeth me beside the still waters. He restoreth my soul; he leadeth me in the paths of righteousness for his name's sake. Yes, though I walk through the valley of the shadow of death, I will fear no evil: for thou art with me; thy rod and thy staff they comfort me. Thou preparest a table before me in the presence of mine enemies; thou anointest my head with oil; my cup runneth over. Surely goodness and mercy shall follow me all the days of my life: and I will dwell in the house of the Lord forever.'* Amen"

"Amen." Taylor followed and looked back up and her mother and Grandmother were now sobbing and holding one another.

"When you are ready to go, I will tell the nurses and they will take Samuel to the morgue to await his transfer to your funeral home."

"Thank you," said Taylor as she nodded. Why had Father Morris picked Psalms 23 to read Taylor thought? Once again there are so many other verses in the Bible, but he read that passage, the exact one Taylor could not get out of her mind.

Olivia and Sarah were the first to leave after saying their goodbyes and Taylor took one last look at the shell of what was her Grandfather. "See you later." Taylor said as she walked out knowing that would be the last time she ever saw Samuel Morgan's body. Samuel had requested cremation and to be put into the lake he spent so much time fishing out of. As a child Taylor and Dawn spent there summers on the lake with their Grandfather. He would take them fishing, swimming, and would even rent jet skis for them to ride. Samuel Morgan hated jet skis. He would often say, "I wish they would build a separate lake for those idiots. They never watch where they are going and they scare the fish."

As Taylor got on to the elevator with her Mother and Grandmother, Dr. Killsmen was standing in the elevator.

He smiled at the women as they got in the elevator with him. "Good morning ladies, how is the patient this morning?" asked Dr. Killsmen.

"He's gone," replied Taylor.

"I am so sorry, I was not notified. Usually I am notified when one of my patients pass."

"It just happened a short time ago."

"Well if there is anything you need just let me know."

"Thank you," Taylor replied. The doors opened and Taylor followed her mother and Grandmother out of the elevator and then stopped and turned to Dr. Killsmen.

"I have a question for you,"

"Yes," replied Dr. Killsmen. Olivia and Sarah were heading down the hallway to the exit and had not noticed Taylor was not behind them.

"Who was the man in the room with my Grandfather when he was here the first time?"

"I don't know if I know whom you are asking about."

"Yes you do, he was another one of your patients that died. My Grandfather watched him die."

"Well, Ms. Bradford, he was not my patient, anyways, I can not tell you his name. Giving out Patient information is against hospital regulations and HIPPA laws."

"It's Mrs. I will find out who he was and at least give his family the truth of how he died."

"Mrs. Bradford, I assure you no good could come of that. Samuel is gone now and he was the only one there that could say how that patient died and he did not come forward when I questioned him about the incident."

"My Grandfather was terrified he would not leave this hospital alive if he told anyone what happened. I am not sick Doctor, so I am not afraid to tell his family."

"I assure you all the steps have been taken to make sure the family knows how that patient died."

"What, complications from surgery?" Taylor replied with a sarcastic tone.

"Whatever the final result was it wouldn't help you. Now go plan your grandfather's funeral."

"I will and then I will be back."

Taylor walked off and passed the desk she passed once before with the same nun sitting there and she looked like she had actually seen the Holy Ghost. She started in amazement as Taylor stormed pass and walked out of St. Anthony's.

The nun's name was Sister Margaret. She had never heard anyone speak to a doctor that way. Dr. Killsmen walked over to the nun's desk and asked what she heard.

"I only heard what you say I heard, Doctor," replied Sister Margaret.

"For now, nothing, Sister," said Dr. Killsmen in his quiet, but affirmative voice.

Ch.16

As Dawn got off the plane and entered the terminal, she saw Kenny waiting for her and he was on his cell phone.

"Are you ok?" asked Kenny.

"Yes, I am just numb. Do you know what I mean?" asked Taylor.

"I think I do, your sister just walked up do you want to talk to her?"

"Yes put her on."

"Taylor, what happened?"

"Grandpa is gone. It happened just about an hour ago. Mom, Grandma and I are on our way to the funeral home in Capespring. We will be there for about an hour or so. Actually, I don't know how long we will be there. I have never planned a funeral before."

"We will go and get my bags and be there as soon as we can."

"I am so happy you are home."

"Me too. See you soon, sis, love ya"

"Bye, love you too, put Kenny back on." Dawn passed the phone back to Kenny and gave him a sad smile.

"Hi, honey," Kenny said.

"Call me when you get close and I will tell you where we are."

"Ok, I love you."

"Love you too, drive careful."

Kenny hung up his phone and grabbed Dawn's carry on and they walked in silence to the luggage claim area.

Ch.17

Taylor pulled into the funeral home parking lot behind her mother and she felt like this was all a dream. Was she really about to enter into a funeral home and plan her Grandfather's final wishes. Taylor walked into the quiet building and was greeted by a very nice older gentleman.

"You must be here for the passing of Samuel Morgan."

Taylor and her mother nodded and Sarah was just standing in the doorway.

"My name is William, but just call me Will.

"Hello, I am Olivia, this is my daughter Taylor and my mother Sarah, Samuel's wife.

"Nice to meet you all let's go into a conference room and discuss the details."

Taylor followed behind her mother and Sarah again.

As they sat down Taylor look around the room. It was bright and very colorful. Not what Taylor had expected a conference room at a funeral home to look like. There were urns in a china cabinet with different books and programs. Taylor wondered why there were no casket pictures to look at on the table or fabric samples. She thought it would be impolite to ask.

"There are a few things we need to discuss, before we talk about burial services or the funeral services." Taylor heard the funeral director start talking as he got out paper and a pen.

"We won't need burial services. Samuel wished to be cremated, " stated Olivia.

"So, we need to go and pick up his remains at the hospital today and get started on the cremation process. I will call the crematorium; I use the one near the hospital, and have them get started right away. Now, what kind of urn would you like?"

"No, urn. We have a box from his tour in Korea we want to use," Olivia answered.

"Ok, how about funeral arrangements."

"We are going to have the services at Taylor's church."

"Alright, I will need that address from you before you leave."

Taylor nodded back at the funeral director.

"How about programs and the obituary?"

Taylor spaced out and started to remember the times she had been to a funeral in the past. Taylor remembered the very first one she could remember and it was when she was five years old and her Great Grandmother had passed away. She remembered walking up to the casket in the front of the very large room. She did not know what she was about to see would stay with her forever. Her Great Grandmother was pale and her eyes were sunken in. Her hands were neatly placed on her stomach and she wore her best Sunday dress. Taylor remembered thinking she looked like she was sick and sleeping very deeply. Then Taylor fast forwarded in time to her friend in high school who died while driving home one night from practice and was hit by a drunk driver. The casket was open and Taylor thought he looked awful and had too much makeup on, but Taylor was crying so much that she could not tell what he was wearing and still to this day can't remember. Then just a few short years later she went to a funeral of one of her cousins on her dad's side She was shot and killed. Taylor remembered her hair looked like it was too big for her head and she looked bigger. Taylor had asked her mom on the way home from the funeral why was her hair so puffy. Taylor's mother told her the funeral home had to make her hair big because, she was shot in the head and they had to cover it up somehow so that people would not notice.

Taylor let out a sigh and came back to the present.

"That is about it. I will bring Samuel's remains to the church on Monday and we will put him in the box you have, before the funeral. If you have any questions here is my card with my cell phone number on it." Olivia took the card and shook his hand and they all stood up.

"Thank you for everything," Olivia said.

As they walked out Olivia told Taylor to come over to her car. Olivia handed her a large shoebox marked pictures.

"Would you put a display of pictures together for Monday we can have on display?"

"Sure, I have a lot of pictures I can add as well."

"What are you going to do now?" Olivia asked.

"Go home and shower and wait for Kenny to get back with Dawn."

"Alright, call me if you need anything. I am going to take Grandma home to get some rest."

Taylor hugged her mother goodbye and waved in the car to her Grandmother who was sitting in the car staring straight ahead.

Ch.18

Taylor's cell phone rang on her way home from the funeral home.

"Hi Honey," said Taylor as she picked up the phone.

"Hi, Dawn and I will be there soon, are you home yet?"

"No, but I will be in a few minutes."

"Meet you there."

"Ok, tell Dawn we have to put together a display of pictures for the funeral on Monday. I will see you soon."

"Bye, love ya."

"Love you too." Taylor closed her phone and sat it in the seat next to her as she thought about how many times she had told Kenny she loved him. She always told him when she was leaving and when they were on the phone. Taylor wanted him to know she loved him and thought about him all the time.

Taylor's phone rang again and Taylor looked at the caller ID and there was only a private number on the display.

"Hello."

"Is this Mrs. Bradford?"

"Yes, who is this?" Taylor knew it was a women and she had a quiet voice she knew from somewhere, but was not sure where.

"I just wanted to tell you to request a copy of all your Grandfather's medical records from the hospital."

"Why?"

"There are some things that are not told to the family members and sometimes they find their way to the medical files. Have a good day."

"Wait who are you?"

The line went silent and Taylor looked at her phone, to see the private caller had hung up. Taylor thought to herself what the woman had said, "There are some things that are not told to the family members and sometimes they find their way to the medical files."

had to be the strangest phone call Taylor had ever gotten. She thought about how she would get the records. Her mother had power to shut off the life support on her Grandfather surely she could sign for the records.

Ch.19

Dr. Killsmen was finishing his shift at the hospital and had seen all of his patients that day and was heading out to his car. Dr. Martin was waiting for him.

"Hello, Doctor."

"Good evening Dr. Martin."

"I wanted to let you know all is well with the Mr. Morgan file and it was taken down to the records department today. I signed off on the Death Certificate and a few last minute reports were done this afternoon. I hope all of yours are transcribed as well."

"Yes, I finished them about 30 minutes ago."

"I look forward to reading them in the morning. Good night Doctor."

Dr. Martin walked away from Dr. Killsmen's car and waved as he entered back into the hospital.

Dr. Killsmen was not paranoid by nature, but he thought it better to look into his car before he unlocked it and got in. There was nothing and no one in the back seat and everything seemed to be as he had left it that morning. He got into the car and turned the key, before doing so he took a deep breath. When the car turned over he let out a loud sigh. Dr. Killsmen wanted more than anything to retire, but he had so much debt, he could not afford to just retire. He thought to himself, maybe I could just up and move to a different city or even a different state. He knew that was not going to be possible for some time, but just the thought made him want to run.

Ch.20

When Taylor got home she showered and put on
some clean clothes and felt like she was like a
brand new person. She had not been home in 2
days and it seemed like weeks.

Taylor sat down in front of the box her mother
had given her marked pictures. She started to
look at the pictures and remembered when some
of them were taken. There were pictures in the
box she did not remember, but all made her
smile. She started at the young man in the
marine uniform and he looked so young and she
thought about all the things that young man had
accomplished and how many people's lives he
had touched. Taylor continued through the box
of pictures and found one she took as a little girl
of her Grandfather sitting in a lawn chair with a
fishing pole in his hands and wearing a
bandana. She remembered he was testing the
line and casting out into the yard and the
chickens from the farm were chasing the rubber
worm on the other end of the line back as he
reeled it in. A tear fell from Taylor's eye and she
wiped it away. There were so many good
memories, how was she going to pick a small
few to display for everyone at the memorial to
look at and share the memories.

Ch.21

Kenny and Dawn pulled in the Driveway and Taylor got up from the couch then walked outside to greet them. Dawn was the first to reach her and gave her a big hug without saying a word.

Kenny walked over to the two women and gave them both a hug. They stood there for what seemed like hours and hugged.

Taylor stepped back and looked at her sister. "You look great."

"You look horrible, but you smell good."

"Thanks a lot, Dawn, I have felt better."

"I think you look wonderful," said Kenny.

"Thank you honey." Taylor turned and kissed Kenny. "Let's go inside."

When the three went into the house Taylor had the pictures of her Grandfather all over the floor.

"I see you have already started," said Dawn.

"Yea, I thought, why wait. I have them in piles by his life. I thought we could do a few bulletin boards. One for his jobs and life before retirement, one for fishing and another for all of the pictures of the family. There are too many to just pick out a few."

"I think it is a great idea," replied Dawn. "I am going to call mom and let her know that I am here and see what she wants to do tonight."

"Alright." As Dawn walked into the other room Taylor pulled Kenny into her arms and he held her tight. "I missed this."

"Me too."

"I wanted to tell you something. I got a strange phone call on my way home from the funeral home. I don't know who it was, but she told me to request Grandpa's medical records."

"Why would you do that?"

"She said that 'There are some things that are not told to the family members and sometimes they find there way to the medical files' what that means exactly I don't know, but I am going to try to get the files."

"Just go to the hospital and have your mother sign for them. She is the next of kin so that should not be a problem."

"I hope it won't be a problem."

Dawn walked back into the room. "I called mom and told her that I would be over soon. Could you give me a ride over there later?"

"Yes, of course, but first let's get to work on these pictures."

Ch.22

Taylor drove Dawn to her Grandmother's house,
where her mother was staying. Taylor told
Dawn about her dream and about Samuel's first
words to her after being unintubated.

"What do you think?"

"Well, Taylor, I don't know. Maybe, Grandpa
going up in flames was just a symbol for him
being cremated and him saying 6,6,6 is just
creepy. I don't have any idea why he would say
that to you, a youth pastor and Christian."

"Well, you are not much help at easing my
mind."

"Sorry, but I love you and I am glad to be
home."

"Me too. I am just going to drop you off I am
not really ready to go into the house yet and
Grandma is still up, so go in and give them my
love and tell mom I will call her tomorrow."

"Ok, but if you need more help call me."

"I will."

Taylor pulled up to the log cabin and Dawn gave her a hug and got out. She opened the back hatch and got her suitcase. "Love you," she yelled as she closed the hatch.

Taylor yelled back, "Love you too sis, good night."

Taylor waved and drove out the driveway. She was expecting to see her Grandfather run out of the woods and stop her and tell her that all of this was a dream and she would wake up soon. That did not happen. Taylor drove home and went into to her quiet small house and saw Kenny waiting for her.

Ch.23

The next day was short for Taylor. She spent the morning and her church planning the memorial for Samuel and talking to her pastor about what she and her family would like done and said.
"Keep it as simple as possible," Taylor told Pastor Jim.
"I have planned a few nice things to say and if you could ask one of your Grandfather's friends to come up and say a few words that would be nice."
"Yes, I will ask one of his fishing buddies to do it. My mom and I decided on 2 songs for the memorial. The first one is 'In the Garden' which you know really well could you sing it?"
"Yes, I would love to that is a good church hymn. What is the second song?"

"Well, it is not exactly a church hymn, but my grandfather loved it. It is a country song by Brad Paisley, 'I'm Gonna Miss Her.' It is funny and my Grandfather thought that it depicted him, when it came to fishing."

"Do you have the CD with you, I would love to hear it."

"Yes, it is in my bag."

Taylor got the CD out of her bag and Pastor Jim put it in the CD player that was wired to the speakers throughout the church. As the song started.

'Well I love her
But I love to fish
I spend all day out on this lake
And hell is all I catch
Today she met me at the door
Said I would have to choose
If I hit that fishin' hole today
She'd be packin' all her things
And she'd be gone by noon'

Pastor Jim started to laugh and Taylor was smiling and crying at the same time. The chorus rang through the church.

'Well I'm gonna miss her
When I get home
But right now I'm on this lakeshore
And I'm sittin' in the sun
I'm sure it'll hit me
When I walk through that door tonight
That I'm gonna miss her
Oh, lookie there, I've got a bite'

By the time the song had ended Taylor was laughing and thinking of her Grandfather stopping the car on the side of the road when this song would come on the radio. She always told him that she would get him a CD player for his old 1976 Suburban, but he always said, "It's better when you hear it on the radio when you aren't expecting it."

Pastor Jim walked over to the CD player and took the CD out and handed it back to Taylor. "I think that is a great song to play in memory of Samuel."

"Thank you. Well I will be bringing all the stuff over early in the morning to set up for the memorial."

"See you then. I will continue to pray for your family."

"Thank you." Taylor hugged her pastor and she began to cry again. "I hope I can get all this out before tomorrow."

"I think it is perfectly normal to cry after losing a loved one that was so close to your heart."

"Yes, but I am dealing with more than just losing my Grandfather. I am worried about where he is now. I can't seem to shake the feeling that I will never see him again."

"Taylor, there is eternal life after death with Jesus."

"I know that, but was my Grandfather offered eternal life?"

"Taylor, only God knows that. Just leave it up to him. Samuel lived a full life filled with love and maybe he found Jesus at the end."

"I hope so."

Ch.24

Sunday night for Dr. Killsmen was always quiet, but it seemed to be even more quiet in his small 2-bedroom apartment than usual. His wife of 25 years had passed away just 2 years earlier of breast cancer and he began drinking and spending all of the money that they had saved for retirement on gambling and alcohol. He was good at keeping his private life separate from his work, but recently he had problems with his conscience. Dr. Killsmen started to drink earlier in the day and was now sitting at his desk with many medical files opened in front of him. He was not sure what to do with them. There was evidence of more than a 100 elderly patients having surgeries and treatments that were unnecessary. All of these patients died untimely deaths due to the extreme procedures that were done on them and Dr. Killsmen, had even been guilty of at least half of the needless procedures, which were supposed to extend a life, but instead killed them. Dr. Killsmen opened a file with the name of Carl Hodges on it and read it aloud. "Cause of death surgical complications following a M.I. and open heart surgery." Then he set it aside and found Samuel Morgan's file. "Cause of death respiratory failure and COPD." The Doctor started at the mountain of files in front of him and thought that he could change a few lives. Give peace where there was anger and resentment. He picked up the 2 medial files and put them in a large a manila envelope. He addressed the envelope and put postage on it and staggered down a flight of stairs and dropped the large envelope in the outside mail depository and ascended the stairs for the last time.

Ch.25

The memorial service was a great tribute to Samuel Morgan and his life. Everyone loved the pictures and the music selection. Taylor and her family spent the afternoon eating and talking about Samuel to his friends and retired colleges. Taylor even learned some new things that she did not know about her Grandfather. "Samuel was always the life of the party, and he always made everyone smile," said one of Samuel's friends that Taylor had not ever met. Taylor thought that she could not say, "Thank you for coming," one more time or she would explode.
She had hugged and shook hands with many people and they all kept saying, "I am so sorry for your loss." Taylor thought that she was blessed to have Samuel as her Grandfather and everyone else was lucky to have known him. She did not feel like she had lost him completely because she still had photos and many memories that she would share with her children if she and Kenny ever had any. No, she did not consider him as gone or like she lost him, but rather he lived on in the things she did and said every day.

Ch.26

The news about Dr. Killsmen's death ran like wildfire on Monday night. The local news report at 6pm stated, "A prominent Doctor from Sunnyville was found dead in his apartment of an apparent over dose of prescription medications and alcohol. There is no evidence of foul play and the police are calling it a suicide. There was a note found next to the body of the Dr. Charles Killsmen. Sources are telling us that the note only said 'I am sorry.' To what that note or whom that note is for is still unknown. Tune in at 10pm for an exclusive with the Doctor that found him after Dr. Killsmen did not show up for his shift at the hospital this morning."

Taylor was listening to the news report and kept staring at the television screen after the news report went to commercial.
"Isn't that Samuel's Doctor?" asked Kenny.
"Yes," replied Taylor as she continued to stare at the screen. The ad was for dishwashing soap and Taylor was watching it as if it was a report of the second coming of Jesus.
"That is crazy," said Dawn who was sitting in the chair next to Taylor.
"I wonder who he is so sorry to, that he would take his own life?" asked Kenny.
"Probably all the families that he has lied to or maybe to God for all the lies and deceit he has brought on by lying to everyone," Taylor said still in amazement.

Ch.27

The next day Taylor went back to work and was calling to all of Samuel's doctors' offices and St. Anthony's trying to get a straight answer on how to get the medical records.

"Why can't you just fax me the form to fill out and then I will have my mother sign it and then you can send the records to me."

"That would be fine Mrs. Bradford, but we need the death certificate and a copy of the power of attorney your mother has over your Grandfather and his affairs," replied a young lady at the records department at St. Anthony's.

"I am sure if you look in his records there is a copy of the power of attorney. My mother had the authority to sign to shut off my Grandfather's life support, I am sure she can sign for medical records."

"May I ask why you are so inclined to get all of the medical records? Don't you just want the reports from the doctors?"

"No, I want everything."

"Well I will send you the form to fill out and have it signed with a copy of the death certificate and power of attorney."

"The death certificate could take weeks to get back from the state."

"Well, I guess you don't mind if I just mail the form then."

"No, I guess it does not matter either way."

Taylor continued to get the same answer from all the offices she called that day.

"How can it be so hard to just get a medical file of someone who is dead?" Taylor asked Kenny that night when she got home from work.

"I don't know honey, but just keep trying and maybe everything will just fall into place. If you were meant to see those records, it will happen."

"How do you always know what to say to make me feel better?"

"It's a gift God gave me so I could make you feel better all the time."

"I love you, I don't know if I say it enough? But I really do love you."

"I love you too, honey."

"Have you seen anything else on Dr. Killsmen and his suicide?"

"Yes, I heard it on the news this morning again and apparently he had some personal problems that may have affected his decision to commit suicide."

"What kind of problems? He always seemed to have it together when I talked to him."

"He had gambling debts and he recently lost his wife to breast cancer."

"He sure did hide that well. I never knew that he had all those problems."

Ch.28

The phone rang at Taylor's office the next morning and Taylor was extremely busy with the children and teens in her church all having problems. Some were having problems with their parents and others with school. Taylor always made sure all of the children in her youth groups knew they could talk to her at any time and about anything. Taylor was an easy person to talk to. Sometimes the pastor of the church would come and sit at her desk and discuss personal problems he had with her. Pastor Jim was a great man and always had a smile on his face to the public, but he had problems just like everyone else. One day he came in and sat down in the chair in front of Taylor's desk and just stared into the space between them. When Taylor had asked, "Are you ok Jim?" He just nodded and said, "I need a few minutes of calm to clear my head."

Taylor said, "Ok, do you mind if I do some work while you clear your head?"

Things were always that way between Pastor Jim and Taylor. He was old enough to be her grandfather and she thought of him as a dear friend. Taylor thought her job of caring for the youth of the church was much easier than caring for the adults in the church. The adults had many, many more problems. The problems of the children and teens were usually temporary and she just had to get them to see past the problem that plagued them now and that it will pass with time. The adult's problems were much larger and much more complicated.

On the 5th ring Taylor answered the phone.

"Did you get the records?" It was the same woman that had called Taylor on the day of her Grandfather's death.

"No, it is more difficult than I expected it to be."

"Keep trying." The phone disconnected.

Taylor called her mother at her grandparents.

"Mom, how long is it going to take to get the death certificate?"

"It could take a few weeks to a few months. Why?"

"I need a copy of it to get the medical records and the power of attorney Grandpa signed."

"Why do you want the records?"

"I just want to see them and read them to understand why we did not get 5 more years with grandpa."

"Taylor it was his time. There was nothing that we could have done or anyone could have done?"

"Maybe," Taylor replied.

Taylor drove home from work that night and thought about the poor man that died in front of her Grandfather. Did his family know what had happened or how he died?

Ch.29

In the large grand conference room at St. Anthony's a dozen doctors, an administrator, and 2 priests sat around a large table. The room was decorated with pictures of Mary and Jesus. Jesus was depicted as a child and in the majority of the pictures he was in Mary's arms. The large table was a dark walnut with matching chairs, which sat 20 comfortably.

The administrator was the head of the hospital; he was neither a doctor nor a man of god; Mr. Adams was simply a businessman. Mr. Adams was a great businessman, but shrewd to the core. He would fire anyone who tried to get in his way of having everything he ever wanted. What Mr. Adams wanted was everything; he had the largest house and the most cars and was always dressed in the finest suits.

The doctors were under the control of the administrator. Dr. Martin was among the doctors at the table. The 2 priests were Father Morris and Father McLaughlin.

The priests were the only ones above the administrator. The priests did not have earthly fortunes or possessions, but they were under the control of the Catholic Church out of New York.

They were given certain presidents over the other priest in the U.S. and had worked hard to become head of the hospital. The New York Catholic Church ran under the direct control of Rome. The Vatican in Italy appointed Mr. Adams the CEO of St. Anthony's. He was highly recommended after the previous CEO had a misfortunate car accident and was brought to St. Anthony's for treatment and died due to injuries sustained in the accident. Mr. Adams was voted in unanimously by the medical staff chiefs, 12 yays and 0 nays.

"What are we going to do with the news coverage we are getting? A doctor from a Catholic hospital committing suicide… Awful. That is not the only problem, people are flooding the phone lines wanting to know what we have to say," said Dr. Martin.

"I want you to all just keep calm. Dr. Killsmen did us a huge favor. His time was up here at the hospital anyways and this saves us a lot of headaches, "said Mr. Adams. "This will all pass and then Dr. Killsmen will be forgotten. I want you to make sure all of Dr. Killsmen files are closed and that you review them and make sure they are all in order."
"Is there anything else that we need to do?" Asked Dr. Martin.
"We need to transfer all of Dr. Killsmen's patients to Dr. Highfill. Dr. Highfill is willing and ready to take over as head of the pulmonology department," replied Mr. Adams.

Ch.30

It was finally Saturday and Taylor had the day off.
She worked 6 days a week. Sunday was her big day
and she had to prepare the lesson for the next Sunday.
She always stayed 1 week ahead. This Saturday was
going to be different. Taylor and her family were
taking Samuel to his final resting place. Samuel
wanted his ashes to be spread on lake where he had
spent so much of his life. Kenny got up early and
went and picked up Samuel's boat and put it in the
water and got it ready to go out for the long journey
to the bluff Samuel pointed out to himself and Taylor
one Saturday. "That is where I want to spend
eternity," Samuel pointed out across the water to the
only large bluff in the whole lake. "I have caught
more fish under that bluff than anywhere else in this
lake; it is only fair that I spend the rest of eternity
lying under that large rock."

Taylor went and picked up her sister, mother and
Grandmother to take them to the boat.
"Do we have everything?" asked Sarah.
"As long as we have Grandpa, I think we have
everything we need," replied Dawn.
"Well, yes, we have Samuel, I think. Olivia, did you
get your father?"
"Yes, Mom I already put him in the car."
"Ok, then let's go," said Taylor.

When they arrived at the dock there was Kenny
standing next to the boat. He had the engine running
and all the seats were cleaned and had cushions on

them. Taylor walked down to the dock and kissed him. "Thank you for all this."

"All what, this is for Samuel. He would not want me to have his boat dirty and have you ladies sitting on the bench seats with no cushions for your bottoms." Taylor laughed and walked on the boat and sat in the Co-Capitan chair next to Kenny. Taylor placed Samuel's ashes on her lap. The day was brisk, but it felt great to be out on the lake. There was no place Taylor like to be more with Kenny. They both loved the water. That was one of things Taylor loved about Kenny, his shared love for the water. As the water splashed past her face and she breathed in the fresh wet air she felt like her Grandfather was there. His remains were there, but it felt like his presence was there and it seemed like there was happiness and peace on the boat. Taylor was picturing him looking down on them all on the boat and smiling, all of his last wishes were being fulfilled.

"We are almost there," Kenny said to Taylor as they rounded a large bend.

Taylor looked up and saw her mother and sister sitting with their arms around Sarah. Samuel's boat was not large but it was sufficient for him and the family to do what they like to do on the lake.

"Who is out there?" Taylor asked Kenny. After they rounded the bend and saw the bluff there were 4 boats sitting in the water bobbing up and down with the waves that they had made.

When Kenny down shifted and coasted towards the bluff the faces of the people on the boats started to come into view. There were about 25 of Samuel's friends. They were fishing buddies and their wives.

Taylor stood up and waved at them. The largest of
the 4 boats had music playing and everyone was
having a good time. Somewhere drinking and others
were fishing and talking to one another.

"What are all of you doing here?" Taylor yelled out to
the boats as they approached.

One of the men yelled back at Taylor. "We wanted to
give Samuel a proper good-bye, the way he would
have liked."

Sarah was waving and saying hello to all of the men
and women on the boats. Taylor knew a few of them,
but was not aware that Samuel had that many friends.
His memorial was very small and not even half of
them had been there.

Kenny anchored the boat and Taylor got Samuel out
of his confining box that he had spent 5 days in. The
bag was large and full of a whitish gray substance,
there was a twist tie holding is shut. Olivia reached
out for the bag of ashes and Taylor handed it to her.

"I think this is the first time I have ever picked Dad
up."

"I know what you mean. It is not a lot of ashes,"
replied Taylor.

Olivia grabbed Sarah by the other hand and guided
her to the bow of the boat.

"Let's just take out a little at time and spread it in
water," Olivia said to Sarah.

As Olivia began to open the twist tie Sarah started to
cry. Olivia held out Sarah's hand and poured a small
amount of ashes into her hand. Everyone on the other
boats was watching and someone started to play
TAPS. TAPS is a military song that is played at
funerals. Taylor knew the song from movies and TV

shows that she had watched. It was appropriate for Samuel. He had been a Marine and a Korean War Vet. Sarah dropped the ashes into the water and then she cried harder and Dawn came up behind her and walked her back to the deck of the boat. Olivia reached into the bag and took out a large handful and said, "Good bye, may you spend eternity with the fish and the water you loved so much."

Taylor came up to the bow of the boat and bent down and hugged her mother. Olivia handed the remaining ashes to Taylor. "You do the rest."

Taylor knelt down and Olivia walked back on to the deck. "Well, it is just you and me again. I miss you so much. I keep thinking that this is all a horrible dream and that you are not really gone forever. I hope that you are spending eternity with Jesus."

Taylor took a small handful of the ashes and spread them across the top of the water and then took a hold of the bottom of the bag and dumped all the ashes into the water. She sat there and watched them go down. She could see them go down further and further into the blackness of the lake. A tear fell into the water after the ashes as if it was following them to the bottom.

Taylor stood up and everyone on the other boats began to clap and a few were even wiping away tears. "Thank you all for coming, I know that it would mean a lot to

Samuel." As Taylor began to go back to the deck a water patrol officer was drifting by. Normally this was not a big deal, but improper disposal of human remains was illegal and

Taylor did not want to go to jail. The man on the larger boat waved at the officer and he waved back and said, "How is everyone doing today?"

"Good. We are just having a small celebration. Care to join us?" replied the man on the large boat.

"No, thanks I have plenty to do myself, but thank you for asking," said the Water patrol officer.

He accelerated his scarab, a fast and efficient boat for chasing anyone who would try to run on the water, and waved.

"That was close. At least we had already put Samuel in the water," said Kenny.

"I bet Grandpa is laughing at us right now, if he saw that," said Dawn.

All of the 5 boats got as close together as they could and tied up together and people were walking across the boats and greeting each other.

"I am sorry that I did not come to the memorial, but churches and funeral don't mix well with me. Some of the others feel the same way so when we found out your family was coming out here today to do this we all decided to come out to pay our respects. I hope you don't mind?" Asked the man that owned the largest boat and saved them from going to jail.

"No, not at all. I am so happy you all came and I know it meant a lot to my Grandmother," said Taylor to the large man as he approached her on Samuel's boat.

Ch.31

Taylor went to bed that night and thought she had fulfilled all of Samuel's last requests. She had a dream that night of Dr. Killsmen.

He was up in the air among the clouds and was kneeling on one of clouds, looking up. Taylor was looking at his face. He looked like he was in agony and his lips were moving, but there was no sound coming from them. Taylor looked up to see what Dr. Killsmen was looking at. She saw a bright light that was gleaming white. It was not like the sun. It was unlike any light she had ever seen.

The light was not in a circular shape, but in a star shaped with beams of light coming from all sides. Taylor looked back down at the Doctor and he was continuing to move his lips, but Taylor could not hear him. Then Taylor heard a voice "You need not hear the words of the damned." Taylor looked back up and saw the light gleam brighter. She thought who was that? "I am the beginning and the end," a voice reverberated to her and through her. Taylor was now kneeling herself and began to pray the Lord's Prayer

"Our Father who aren't in heaven, hollowed be thy name. Thy kingdom come, thy will be done on earth as it is in heaven. Give us this day our daily bread. Forgive us our debts, as we forgive our debtors. And lead us not into Temptation, but deliver us from evil. For thine is the Kingdom and the power and the glory forever. Amen."

Taylor woke up to Kenny shaking her. "Wake up Taylor your dreaming."
"What," Taylor was waking up from her dream.
"You're praying in your sleep."
"I was?"
"Yes, I woke up at *'And lead us not into Temptation'*"
"Sorry, I had the weirdest dream."
Taylor told Kenny of her dream. "Maybe you were visiting the 'good doctor's' judgment."

"I don't know why I dreamt that, but I remember that the light was warm and made feel love and happiness. Dr. Killsmen did not even see me and he did not look as though he was having a good time."

"I would bet not. I don't think God looks to kindly on suicide."

"Or lying," replied Taylor.

Taylor went back to sleep and slept dreamlessly the rest of the night.

Ch.32

Sunday morning was the same as always. The congregation said a short prayer for Taylor and her family for the loss of Samuel. Taylor was a little sheepish at the prayer for Samuel. She did not know if this was something that was really necessary. She had dreamed of Dr. Killsmen's judgment, if Kenny was right, but not Samuel's. Samuel had already had his judgment and was spending eternity where God saw fit; it was already too late for him.

Taylor came home from church and Kenny was home from fishing. "How was church?"
"Fine, it would have been better if you were there.'
"I had church out on the lake today. You should have been there. The birds were singing hymns."
"Yeah, yeah, you had fun."

"Yep, the mail is on the desk. There is a lot. We should really go through it more often than once a week."

"I don't have time to go through it every day. Is there anything good?"

"I don't think so, there are some cards, I assume sympathy cards, and bills. One large envelope with no return address for you."

"Did you open it?"

"No, you know I don't like to open mail. It is always depressing, all those bills."

Taylor walked into the office that she and Kenny shared. There was a small desk with a computer and a printer on it. Stacked in the middle of the desk was a large stack of envelopes.

Taylor let out a loud sigh; Kenny heard it in the living room and laughed.

She sat down and started to go through the mountain of papers. She said allowed as she sorted, "bill, bill, bill, junk mail, more junk, card from your mother, card from your father, and large envelope. This envelope has a lot of postage stamps on it. I bet it weighs a few pounds."

Kenny yelled back from the couch, "I thought it was big and why didn't they take it to the post office and have it weighed."

Taylor opened the envelope and slid the pages out of it. The top of the first page said Samuel Morgan ID# 1097786. There were lab reports and history and physical reports, OP notes, Procedure notes, all with doctors' names on the reports. Then Taylor fingered through the pages. Carl Hodges ID # 1097654 was at the top of one of the reports. Who is Carl Hodges? Taylor thought to herself? She continued to look at his records; the same was in there, all of his lab reports, history and physical reports, OP notes, and procedures notes. "Kenny, could you come here?"

"What is wrong?" Taylor handed Kenny the stack of papers she got in the mail. He looked through them and looked in astonishment.

"Who sent these to you?"

"I don't know, there is no note or return address."

"What is the date on the envelope?" Kenny put the papers down and looked at the envelope.

"This is dated the day after Dr. Killsmen died."

"Do you think he sent this?" asked Taylor as she started to look at the paperwork again.

"Probably, or he had someone send it."

Taylor began to go through the pages one at a time. What she did not understand she looked up on the internet. She saw Samuel had an infection in his blood and in his urine that had been called staphylococcus. *More than 100,000 in every specimen.* Taylor noticed that the date on the first test was right before Samuel came home. 5 days before he died. There was another blood test drawn, upon arrival at St. Anthony's, when he flew in by Life Line. The test was ordered by the attending ER physician. The lab technicians reached the same result a second time. Samuel was riddled with a bacterial infection that was not treated. Taylor began looking up staphylococcus infections on the internet. All the websites she looked at said the same thing. If a staphylococcus infection is not treated eventually death is inevitable. Taylor continued to look through the pages. The Operation note from the first time Samuel was admitted was from a lung biopsy. Dr. Killsmen had performed the procedure and it seemed that nothing had been noted to be wrong. There was a pathology report attached to the OP note. Normal lung tissue was at the bottom of the report. Taylor looked at the report and normal lung tissue once again. If Samuel had normal lung tissue, why would they diagnosis him with COPD, Taylor thought to herself. As Taylor continued to look through the medical papers she began to understand more and more of the medical lingo. Samuel's chest X-ray from his initial trip to the hospital read he had pneumonia in the lower left lobe.

Taylor picked up the medical file with Carl Hodges on the outside of the file. She did not know what exactly she was looking for. The first page had his address and his emergency contact information on it. It read: Carl Hodges 112 N. Division Street Sunnyville, KS,. Emergency contact Diana Hodges, wife, 658-425-9206.

Could it be that easy, just a phone number and an address to the one person she wanted to talk to. It was all in front of her, at her fingertips. Taylor continued to look at the paper work and there was a copy of the affidavit signed by Dr. Martin, cause of death: complications post OP.

Taylor took a deep breath and sat back in her office chair. She looked up and saw Kenny still standing in the office. "I forgot you were still here," she said in a tired voice.

"I figured, you were reading so intently that I did not want to bother you. Did you learn anything new?"

"Apparently, Grandpa had an infection in his blood and in his urine. The X-rays of his lungs showed clouding thought to be pneumonia by the radiologist, but needed additional work up for diagnosis."

"Well that could explain a lot of problems he was having, before he went into the hospital."

"I think he got the infection in his blood and in his urine in the hospital and just had pneumonia when he had the shortness of breath," replied Taylor. "What am I going to do with all this information?"

"I don't know, but you wanted it and now it is right here."

"I know, but should I call Mrs. Hodges and tell her what I know? I don't know her and is she really going to believe me?"

"Why don't you just sleep on it tonight and maybe tomorrow you will know what to do?" Kenny put his hand out and Taylor laid the papers on her desk and took Kenny's hand and went to bed. She did not fall asleep right away she prayed and then asked for guidance on what to do next. Kenny was sound asleep next to her and she began talking in a hushed tone. "Dear God, help me to make the right choices. I am asking you for your help in choosing the right path." Then Taylor fell asleep.

Ch.33

Mr. Adams was working in his office when the door suddenly crept open. "Mr. Adams, can I talk to you?" It was the quiet nun from the check in desk Sister Margaret.

"Can it wait Sister I am in the middle of doing some paperwork?"

"No, I don't think it can." Sister Margaret was usually a meek person that did not interfere with the workings of the hospital. She lived in a small room in the nearby convent with 30 other nuns and she liked her job and helping others.

"Come in, Sister." Mr. Adams stood up and then he walked over to the other side of his desk and gestured for her to take a seat. "What do I owe this honor to?"

"Well, it is about Dr. Killsmen. I overheard him getting into a confrontation with a family member about the death of another patient. Not her Grandfather, but she wanted the name of a patient that had passed away and apparently her Grandfather witnessed his death."

"What did Dr. Killsmen tell this woman?"

"He did not say anything. He just told her it was against HIPPA laws to give out the names of patients living or deceased. What is bothering me is that she said that her Grandfather feared for his life while in this hospital."

"What was this woman's name?"

"Mrs. Bradford. Her Grandfather was Samuel Morgan. He died about a week ago."

"Have you told anyone else about this, Sister?" Mr. Adams was now sitting on the corner of his desk and looking down at Sister Margaret.

"No, just Dr. Killsmen. He told me to not say anything."

"Well that was good advice. I want you to forget about it all, and just go back to your station." Sister Margaret began to get up out of the chair and looked at Mr. Adams face. He had a smile on that would have impressed the devil.

"Is there something else, Sister?"

"No, I just was hoping Dr. Killsmen did not commit suicide over this."

"I know that Dr. Killsmen was a respected doctor and was well liked by the staff, but he had more problems than anyone could possibly know."

"Thank you for explaining things and God bless you, Mr. Adams."

"And you, Sister."

When Sister Margaret had exited the office, Mr. Adams walked over to the other side of his desk and sat down and picked up the phone.

Ch.34

When Taylor got to work the next morning she made copies of the files she brought with her. She was afraid to leave them anywhere. She thought that if she left them, they would disappear. Taylor was busy making the copies when Pastor Jim came in.

"Good Morning, Taylor."

"Hello, how are you today?"

"I am doing well Mrs. Marks is in the hospital, so I am going to make a trip up to Sunnyville. Do you want a ride with me?"

"Sure, let me finish these copies." Taylor did not stop copying and she did not even realize what she had agreed to at first. "St. Anthony's, is that where Mrs. Marks is?"

"Yes, she had a small stroke last night and Mr. Marks called me this morning. She is going to be fine, praise Jesus, but I would like to go and see her."

Mr. and Mrs. Marks had been church members for over 20 years and were very active in the church. "Well I am glad that she is going to be ok. Would you do me favor and hold on to this envelope for a while? Just lock it up in your desk and I will let you know if I need it."

"Of course, but what is it?"

"Just some important papers that I want to have more than one copy of." Pastor Jim took the large envelope and then put it in his desk drawer and locked it. He turned and looked at her and realized that she looked older than he remembered. Taylor Bradford had always had a youthful appearance and that is why the youth seemed to bond with her more than the much older Pastor Jim. She was pretty and she always looked nice in her more modern look than the rest of the adults at the church. The majority of the small congregation was traditional and did not care what the latest fashions were. Taylor and the youth were always up on the newest looks and that is why Pastor Jim hired Taylor. She was a good person and always did everything to help the youth and Pastor Jim.

"Are you ready to go?"

"Yes, let me just get my bag." Taylor put the copies of the records she had into her bag and followed Pastor Jim out to his car. Pastor Jim had an old car that he refused to trade in. It was 7-year-old dodge neon. Taylor always told him that he should trade it in for something more modern, but he liked it and was not big on change.

"How is your family doing?"

"Oh, they are dong ok. My Grandmother is driving my mom crazy. Her dementia is getting worse and she does not always remember that Grandpa is gone. Mom hates to explain his death to her over and over, but they are doing fine otherwise."

"That is too bad, but I suppose that is to be expected after your Grandfather's death."

"We did not expect Grandma to be as bad as she is. Grandpa always said that she was getting forgetful, but he was always home with her and was like her memory. Without him she cannot remember anything."

"I am glad your Mother is able to take care of her. How is Kenny?"

A smile went across Taylor's face at the mention of Kenny's name. "He is good. We are thinking of expanding our family in the next couple of years. He is working a lot of hours with the construction business and new homes are going up every week. I just wish he had more time to work on our house."

"They say that a mechanic never has time to work on their own car and it is similar."

"Yea, I guess." Taylor looked out the passenger window and thought about Kenny and their life. It has been a difficult and bumpy ride, but he has always been there for her and she loved him more than anything in this world.

As they pulled into the parking ramp at St. Anthony's Taylor remembered the last time she was there and drove away leaving Samuel there and the fear and resentment she felt toward the hospital.

Ch.35

Pastor Jim went up to the desk and asked for room number for Mrs. Marks. Taylor waited by the entrance door and looked down the long hallways. Nothing had changed in the last week since Taylor had been there. There were still nurses and doctors walking up and down the halls with patient's being guided or wheeled around.

"This way Taylor," Pastor Jim said to Taylor waking her from her daze.

"I will follow you." They went up the elevator to the same floor Samuel was on and into the ICU. Taylor looked into the room she spent the worse days and nights of her life in, and there was a child in the room with machines hooked up to him. Taylor saw the same nurses she knew from her Grandfather's stay in the ICU. Then she looked around and saw a man looking at her intently as if he knew her. No one else was paying any attention to her, but this man was looking at her as if she was a wearing a sign on her face that said stare at me. The man was wearing an all-black suit with a grey tie that was neatly tied. He stood behind the nurse's station, and had his hands in his pockets and was leaning against the back wall. Taylor followed Pastor Jim into a room where Mrs. Marks was lying in bed and Mr. Marks was sitting in the chair next to her holding hand

"Hello, Pastor and Taylor, it is good to see you both," said Mr. Marks as the two entered the small glass room.

"Hello, Mr. Marks. How is the patient doing this morning?"

"She's doing well. The doctor came in earlier and said that she should be transferred to another room and on another floor."

"That is great," said Pastor Jim.

"I hope that they are treating you good here," said Taylor.

"Yes, yes all the nurses have been nice and a priest came in and prayed with us. I told him we weren't catholic, but he said that is ok, as long as we all believe in Jesus."

"I do believe that is true. Would you mind if I said a little prayer also?" Asked Pastor Jim.

"Yes, please do," said Mrs. Marks in a quiet voice.

"Would you excuse me for a minute?" Asked Taylor. "I have something I would like to do before we go."

"I did not realize my sermon's bothered you so much."

"No, that is not it. I will meet you out at the car." Taylor said her goodbyes to Mr. and Mrs. Marks and left the glass room. She went out to the hallway and looked for the man she saw when she came in, but he was gone. Taylor walked up to nurse's desk and saw an older lady sitting there. "Did you see where the man in the black suit with the gray tie went?"

"What man?" Asked the older lady.

"He was standing back there," Taylor pointed to the back of the nurse's station. "And he was leaning against the back wall."

"I am sorry. I did not see anyone." Taylor looked at the woman and shook her head and turned around. Taylor saw a man in a black suit walk out the doors of the ICU and into the main hallway. Taylor followed him out and looked down the hallways and saw him enter another room. Taylor did not know if the man saw her trailing him, but she continued on down the hallway after him. The door closed behind the man. Taylor saw the sign above the door and it said stairway. Taylor opened the door and looked up and down the stairs and listened to see if she heard footsteps in either direction. She heard the heavy footsteps going up the stairway and she trailed behind with quiet steps. Taylor did not want to make a noise that would give her position away. Taylor did not know where the steps lead, but she knew eventually she would end up on the roof of the hospital. She had started out on the fifth floor and was going up quietly and did not hear any doors open and close ahead of her. She could still hear faint footsteps above her.

The man in the grey suit knew Taylor was behind him. He did not know how close behind, but he had heard the door faintly open and close after he had closed it behind him. When he reached the top of the stairs he opened the heavy metal door that had a sign on it roof access. The door was supposed to remain locked at all times, but it had been unlocked in the last hour. The black suited man was not at all worried that Mrs. Bradford would catch up with him. He was waiting for it.

Taylor heard the door at the top of the stairs open and close. She was not sure if she had been heard or if the man knew she was behind him. She opened the door as quietly as she could and looked out before crossing the threshold and stepping on to the rooftop. She could see only large fans and vents with hot steam coming out of them. There was no one in her view. She crossed the threshold and made a soft step on to the gravel top. The man in the black suit was directly behind the door and as soon as Taylor stepped on the roof she was immediately aware she had made a huge mistake.

The man in the black suit put his arms around Taylor and covered her mouth with his large hands. He was at least a foot taller than Taylor and he easily over powered her with one swoop of his arm.

"I want you to listen very carefully. I was made aware you are questioning this hospital and some of the care of the patients. I would like you to stop. Dr. Killsmen is gone and we would like to close the book on all of this. Mrs. Bradford, are you listening to me?"

Taylor could not respond verbally, but nodded her head up and down.

"Stop, investigating or looking in to things, whatever you think you were doing, you will stop. I am going to take my hand off of your mouth and I don't want you to scream. If you scream we will have to resume this awkward position."

Taylor nodded her head up and down and mumbled, "I won't scream." Taylor had begun to ask herself why had she followed this man and what had possessed her to come on to the roof. The man in the black suit took his hand off of her mouth and then turned her around with his other hand. Taylor looked up and realized that the man was older and had a large scar over his right eyebrow. He had dark hair and was looking directly into her eyes. She had a look of panic and shock in her eyes that was apparent to the man.

"I am not going to hurt you. Do you understand?"

"Yes." Taylor did not think that she should disagree with the man. She was alone and had no weapon and this man could kill her with one hand. Taylor became acutely aware that she had her bag on her arm and it was falling. She remembered that she had but the medical files in her bag and she looked down only for second and the man in the black suit was aware that she looked down to her bag. He let go of the arm holding the bag, and her tote fell to the ground and papers were strung about the gravel. The black suited man saw that her face was showing a new level of panic.

"Is there something in your bag you would like to tell me about?" Taylor shook head no vigorously and looked directly into his eyes.

"Are you sure? You seem to be upset that your bag is on the ground." Taylor continued to shake her head no.

"Well I guess you don't mind if I take a look then. Do you?" The man reached down with his free hand and pulled Taylor with his other by her small bicep. Taylor was now feeling pain where his grip had become tight. She knew he was leaving finger marks on her skin.

"Please, don't look in my bag." Taylor began to beg. She was not one for begging, but she did not want the man to see the papers that were in her bag. She knew if he saw them she would have a lot of explaining to do. He picked up the papers that had fallen onto the gravel and began to read the top page.

"Well, well, what do we have here?" Taylor began to panic and she started to flail and kick the man. She did not know how she was going to get away, but knew she either had to fight or give up. She was not ready to give up.

"Are you really going to try to get away?" The man said and started laughing. In one swoop he grabbed her under her other arm and lifted her off the ground. Taylor was still flailing about and began yelling.

"Help, someone!"

"No one can hear you up here." The man said as he carried Taylor over to the edge of the roof. "Do you want to fall of the roof? No one will question your death. You committed suicide at the exact place your grandfather died and you just could not go on; you were so sad."

"I don't want to die! Please put me down. I will stop," Taylor pleaded.

"I will let you go one more time and you will listen and answer some questions." Taylor nodded in agreement. He put her down on the gravel.

"What do you want to know?"

"Where did you get these?" The man still had the medical files in his hand and held them up so Taylor was eye level with them.

"They were sent to me."

"By whom?"

"I don't know."

"Really, you don't know."

"No, I am not sure who sent them, but I got them in the mail and the envelope was addressed to me."

"Well, I am going to have to figure that out. We don't want medical records just getting sent out to people." The man walked back over to Taylor's bag and had a hold of her arm again. He picked it up and emptied the entire contents on to the ground. All of the papers were now exposed among her wallet and make up and her bible. The man bent over and through her bag to the side. He picked up all of the paperwork.

"Who are you?" Taylor asked feeling braver now that she had been spared from sure death.

"I am the muscle of this whole hospital. No one and nothing gets passed me. I know everything about this hospital and what goes on with in its walls. You can call Mr. Calvin." Mr. Calvin got into his jacket pocket and pulled out his cell phone. "I have a call to make, do not move."

Taylor looked at Mr. Calvin and said, "A phone call? Who are you calling?"

"Well that is none of your business. Just keep quiet and don't move or we will visit the edge again."

Taylor did as she was told and looked down to all of her things that were on the ground and her cell phone was face up and she could see that she had missed 4 calls. She thought that Kenny or Pastor Jim must have been trying to get a hold of her. She had put her phone on vibrate when she went into the hospital. Now she wished she had put her phone in her pocket and not her tote bag.

"It's me, boss. Yes, I have talked to her and she has some medical files with her. One is on Samuel Morgan and the other is Carl Hodges." Mr. Calvin was listening to the other voice on the line and he was staring at Taylor the entire time not taking his eyes off of her. "Yes, I know that." He said into the phone. "I will make sure. Yes she is aware of the importance. Yes, boss." Mr. Calvin hung up the phone and placed it back into his pocket. "Well, today is your lucky day, Mrs. Bradford. I am going to leave you here, but remember that I am always watching and I know everything."

"How did you know I was here today?"

"That is a good question. This hospital is completely covered by surveillance cameras and you were spotted upon entry. I was notified that you were on the premises and were you were going. I saw you enter the ICU and I went in the doctors entrance and waited for you. The rest you did on your own. Remember Mrs. Bradford you are going to forget this ever happened and do not try to pursue this quest you feel obligated to fulfill. Mr. Hodges and Mr. Morgan will still be dead and nothing you do can change that now."

"I know that, Mr. Calvin." Taylor said in a sarcastic tone.

"Don't forget your things, Mrs. Bradford. I hope I never see you again." Mr. Calvin walked back towards the door that Taylor had entered only a short while ago and was ambushed.

Taylor bent down and picked up her tote bag and picked up her cell phone. She saw Pastor Jim had called twice and Kenny had called the other 2 times.

Ch.36

Mr. Calvin walked directly from the rooftop to the parking garage where Pastor Jim was sitting in the car waiting for Taylor. He was sitting in the car and was reading his bible and singing. Mr. Calvin walked past the small neon and continued to the back of the parking lot so he would not be seen. He saw Taylor walk into the garage and saw she was holding her upper arm and rubbing it. He did not realize he had used so much force on her. He did not like to hurt people as a rule, but only when it was necessary. Taylor got into the neon and Pastor Jim turned the engine over and they drove away. Mr. Calvin watched as they pulled out of the garage and into traffic. He pulled his cell phone back out and hit redial. "Yea, she left. No there was no problems. I will bring you all the records she had. No, I did not make sure she had not made copies. She was really worried about me finding these. I don't think she made copies."

Ch.37

"You, need to call the police, Taylor," Kenny said, when he got home from work, after Taylor had told him what had happened at the hospital. "No, that is not what I am going to do. I am going to do the opposite of what they want." Taylor had just gotten out of a hot shower and was in her bathrobe. When she pulled it off to get dressed Kenny saw the bruises on her arm. "What did he do to you?" Kenny asked in a concerned voice and walked over to her to look at the bruises more closely.

"They are ok, they don't even hurt." As she said it Kenny took his hand and brushed the bruises. "Ouch. Well, they don't hurt as much." Taylor took her arm and grabbed it and rubbed the bruises.

"You should put some ice on those. Your arm is swollen and the finger prints are really black."

"Yea, maybe that is a good idea. I am going to get dressed and make us some dinner."

"I think you need to call the police, but you don't seem too interested in what I think."

"I am going to call Mrs. Hodges and tell her about her husband's death tomorrow."

"I thought the man in the black suit took the records?"

"Mr. Calvin, yes he took the ones that were sent to me, but I made copies this morning. Pastor Jim has them locked up in his desk at the church." Taylor was getting dressed in sweats and was starting to feel like a whole person again. That was making her more determined to do what she thought was right.

"You are sneaky." Kenny gave Taylor a sly smile. "I hope Mrs. Hodges doesn't call the hospital and verify your claims when you call her. That would really make someone mad at the hospital."

"I don't think she will, at least I hope she does not call, at least not right away."

"Who do you think is in charge of Mr. Calvin? Who did he call when you were up on the roof?"

"I don't know, but whoever it is, has no fears about killing people."

"That is why I want you to call the police. I don't want to lose you." Kenny walked over to Taylor and wrapped his arms around her.

"Would you please carry the mace can I got you a few years ago? It may not hurt anyone, but it would give you enough time to get away." Taylor nodded her head and kissed Kenny.

Ch.38

Mr. Adams was in his office late and not in a good mood. He was typing on his computer and working on the finances of the hospital. Mr. Adams had a way of working numbers. If the hospital could prolong the life of one insured patient by a week, by doing tests and performing procedures he could gain up to $100,000.00. He loved numbers and especially numbers with a lot of zero's behind them.

He had a file come across his desk today of a 55 year old male who was to undergo a quadruple bypass to unclog his arteries. The 55-year-old man was not stable enough to undergo such a surgery so close to a myocardial infarction, but the cardiologist told the family he would die without the surgery. So the man and his wife agreed to the man having surgery. While in the operating room the man coded after only 2 of the bypasses were completed. It took the cardiologist 20 minutes to get the man's heart beating again

When he came out of surgery he had to be put on a ventilator and then a feeding tube. The doctors told the wife that he could not be woke up and had to be sedated so he would not fight the tubes. The man never woke up after he was sedated before the surgery. Mr. Adams had to decide how long the doctors where going to keep him on life support and run more neurological tests to see if he was brain dead. The initial reports in front of him said that the man had no neurological activity. The man's wife was not told this. She was told that he needed time to recover and he could wake up at any time. Mr. Adams was calculating the amount he could gain from the insurance company if the doctors and machines kept the man alive for at least a week. Mr. Adams loved to play god with the patients and deciding when they should expire. Occasionally, the patients would not wait until the opportune time and die on their own. Mr. Adams did not like this; he would rather tell the doctors when it was time for them to expire. Mr. Adams did not have much resistance from the doctors. Dr. Killsmen had protested one too many times and Mr. Adams knew he paid the price.

Ch.39

The next morning Taylor woke up and was still in a daze, thinking about the day before and everything that had happened. She knew what she had to do and how to do it, but she did not know what the ramification would be.

Taylor got up and turned on the coffee. Kenny was still asleep and she knew he had to be at work soon, but she did not want to wake him. She took her shower and got dressed to go to the church. When she came out of the bathroom Kenny was standing there with a cup of coffee for her.

"Are you still going to call Mrs. Hodges today?"

"Yes, I am."

"I was hoping that after you slept on it, you would have changed your mind."

"No, sorry. I am still going to call her. I don't know what will follow or what she will say, but I prayed on it and I still believe I am doing the right thing." Taylor had made up her mind and she had that to a fault. Whenever she decided she was going to do something she did it.

"Well, I am glad that you prayed on it. I hope you prayed for our safety and your life."

"Of course, I did. I know that god will watch over me."

"Watch, I want him to protect you. Send a few angels to defend you if need be."

Taylor gave Kenny a smile and she nodded and walked over and hugged Kenny. He went to shower and get ready for work. Taylor called Pastor Jim.

"Good morning Taylor," said Pastor Jim. "To what do I owe this?"

"Do you remember yesterday I gave you some papers to hold on to? Well, I need them."

"That was not very long. I thought I was holding them for something important."

"You were, but something happened to my originals and I need the copies."

"I will be in the office later this morning and I will get them for you."

"Great, I will see you soon."

Ch.40

Taylor waited at the church office with anticipation she was eager now to call Mrs. Hodges. She worked on her sermon and she tried to do some paperwork, but she was distracted. She was contemplating what she was going to say to Mrs. Hodges. She did not want to sound like a crazy person, but she wanted Mrs. Hodges to understand the seriousness of the situation and yet to be understanding of her loss.

"Taylor, how are you this morning?" asked Pastor Jim as he came in.

"I am fine."

"You seem distracted. Is there something that you would like to talk about?"

"Yea, maybe soon, I have something I need to do first. I don't want anyone trying to talk me out of it. Kenny has already tried."

"I assume that this is about the papers in my desk?"

"Yes."

"Well, let's get you started." Pastor Jim walked over to his desk and took his keys out and unlocked the drawer and he looked in the drawer. Taylor was waiting in front of his desk and was getting scared. She thought for only a split second that the papers were gone. Had the hospital found out she made copies and had someone break into the church and steal the copies of the medical records.

"Well I know that I put them in here," said Pastor Jim. "Oh, here they are."

Taylor reached out and grabbed the envelope and opened it. She wanted to see the papers, make sure they were still in the envelope. When she took them out she let out a sigh of relief. They were all still there.

"I am glad you are happy to see them. What are they?"

"Pastor, they are worth killing over."

Pastor Jim looked at Taylor and said, "Well, I am glad I don't have them anymore."

"I am glad I made copies yesterday. Can I have the office for a few minutes?"

"Sure, I am going to have breakfast with the board of directors and I won't be back until lunch."

"Then I will see you later," Taylor sat in Pastor Jim's chair at his desk and started going through the records. She came to Mr. Hodges record and his next of kin was right there along with the address and phone number.

Taylor picked up the phone and began to dial. She prayed one more time as she was dialing. "Dear Lord please let this be the right thing to do. Please let everything workout and be ok." The phone rang 2 times and a woman picked up. "Hello."

"Mrs. Hodges?" Taylor asked.

"Yes, who is this?"

"My name is Taylor Bradford and you don't know me, but my grandfather knew your late husband."

"Oh, well that is nice. Who is your Grandfather?"

"He was Samuel Morgan. He passed away a few weeks ago, at St. Anthony's."

"I am so sorry. I know losing a loved one is difficult."

"Yes, that is why I am calling."

"Ok, I lost my husband recently."

"I know my grandfather was there when your husband died."

"Really, the hospital said he died in his sleep after surgery."

"Did the hospital tell you anything else?"

"No, Dr. Martin was his primary care physician and he called me the morning Carl died. He said that the nurses went in to do morning rounds and he had died during the night."

"Mrs. Hodges, I am going to tell you the story my grandfather told me about your husband's death. I want you to remember that I have nothing to gain from this. I thought that you would want to know the truth."

"Of course, I do, but how do I know you aren't lying?"

"You will have to trust me."

"Tell me what happened and I will decide that after I hear what you have to say.' Mrs. Hodges took a seat at her kitchen table. She was listening intently to Taylor's account of what happened to her husband.

"My Grandfather did not tell anyone, but me. He was afraid someone at the hospital would kill him. He was scared."

"Well, that is a terrifying story. I don't believe the nurses at the hospital would just let someone lie in bed and bleed to death. That is what you are telling me?"

"Yes, that is what I am telling you. I also want to tell you that the hospital is not innocent. I was threatened by the hospital to drop all of it, to just forget everything I knew."

"How did you get my phone number?"

"I have some of Mr. Hodges medical record. It was sent to me in with my Grandfather's record."

"Who sent them to you?" Mrs. Hodges was now thinking that Taylor was a crazy thief that stole medical records on deceased patients and called the widows to scam them.

"I don't know. The envelope did not have a return address and no note. I think a doctor from the hospital sent them to me."

"Why don't you just ask this doctor if they sent them to you?"

"The doctor I think sent the records to me is now dead."

"That is sure convenient, isn't it?"

"No, not really. Dr. Killsmen killed himself the day of my Grandfather's funeral."

"I saw that on the news. That was sad. What did you mean that you were threatened?"

Taylor told Mrs. Hodges what happened on the roof at the hospital. She did not go into great detail as she had done about her husband's death. Taylor wanted her to realize how important this information was.

"I want you to know that I am available to you, anytime you want to talk," Taylor said. Taylor gave Mrs. Hodges her cell phone number and she said she had the number to the church from the caller ID.

Taylor hung up with Mrs. Hodges and felt like she had done something to accomplish her goal. She had not brought down the hospital or exposed their faults to the world, but she had changed the life of one family. She hopped that Mrs. Hodges had believed her, and not thought she was a loon.

Ch.41

Kenny went to work that day and felt like he had to do something about Taylor. He wanted to protect her from anyone that would harm her, which included a hospital. He was not concerned about rising flags or causing the hospital to have bad publicity. Kenny had a friend that he went to school with that was now a police officer in the town they lived in. Kenny called him first thing that morning and told him what had happened to Taylor.

"I know this all sounds crazy, but Phil, it is all happening. The threats are real. Taylor had bruises on her arm where the man had held her."

"Kenny, there is nothing that can be done if Taylor is not willing to come forward and fill out a complaint."

"Taylor is not going to do that she is determined to see this through. Today she called the widow of the man her Grandfather witnessed die in his hospital bed."

"What?" said Officer Phil Grover.

"Yea, she feels more determined since the hospital had that thug threaten her."

"Kenny, the only thing I can tell you is to be more vigilant about your surroundings and I will keep an eye on your home. I will have a patrolman drive by once a shift."

"Thank you and I will try to convince Taylor to come in and fill out a report." Kenny knew that would not happen. He knew Taylor better than anyone else and he knew when she had her mind made up, she was almost always unmovable.

"Let me know if there is anything else I can do for you or Taylor."

"Thanks Phil." Kenny hung up and felt like he accomplished nothing and was not going to tell Taylor that he called Phil. He did not want to upset her or make her think he did not trust her judgment.

Ch.42

Mr. Adams was working in his office that morning and was not expecting the phone call from Dr. Martin.

"Good morning Doctor. What can I do for you?"

"We have a problem."

"Oh really, what problem is that?"

"Carl Hodges wife called my office this morning and demanded I call her back about her husband's death. So, I called her and she says that our young Mrs. Bradford called her today and told her how her husband really died. She also says that Mrs. Bradford was attacked at the hospital and told not to pursue what her grandfather, Mr. Morgan, had seen."

"This is all very interesting, Dr. Martin. I am glad that you called me. I will take care of this. What did you tell Mrs. Hodges?" Mr. Adams was now angry. He thought that Mr. Calvin had taken care of this, apparently not.

"I told her Mrs. Bradford was going through severe grief and loss issues due to the recent loss of her Grandfather and she was not in her right mind. I convinced her that Mrs. Bradford is a little crazy."

"Do you think she believed you?"

"Yes, I do. She is completely gullible. She is a nice enough lady, but not much upstairs."

"That is good."

"What are you going to do about Mrs. Bradford?"

"Don't worry about that. She was told what would happen if she pursued this quest of hers."

"Are you going to kill her too?"

"I don't think you should worry about that, have a good day." Mr. Adams hung up his office phone and picked up his cell phone that was on his desk. He scrolled through his list of numbers until he found the one he was looking for. The phone rang on the other end of the line and then a loud beep. Mr. Adams left a message.

"Mr. Calvin I need to see you in my office now." Mr. Adams did not need to leave his name. He knew Mr. Calvin would know who he was from his voice.

Ch.43

When Taylor got home from work that night Kenny was already home and Dawn was there. She was leaving the next morning for Alabama. She had spent as much time as she could in Kansas and needed to get home. Dawn was missed by her boyfriend and she was ready to go back to her home.

Kenny was grilling out and Dawn was spending her last night with them and Taylor was going to drive her to the airport in the morning.

"I am sure going to miss you sis," Dawn said to Taylor while they were setting the table for dinner.

"I am going to miss you too. I hope you get to come back soon."

"I will. I am not going to stay away as long as I did before. I regret not seeing Grandpa for a couple of years."

"He knows you had your own life to live. He was not mad that you did not make it to see him before he died. What matters is you were here for all of us after he died and you stayed to help Mom with Grandma."

"I know, but I still wish I could have said goodbye," Dawn said as a tear fell. Taylor walked over and gave her sister a hug.

"You told him goodbye at the lake. That is what matters."

"Yea, I guess you are right. I am sure he knows I was there."

"I believe he knows we were all out there on the lake, fulfilling his last wishes."

Kenny came in with a plate full of steaks.

"Dinner is ready!" Kenny said as he sat down with the plate of steaks in front of him.

"I hope you don't think you are only eating steak for dinner," said Taylor as she smiled at him.

"If I had it my way, yes, but I am sure you are going to make me eat vegetables."

"Of course, we are having broccoli and potatoes with the steak," said Taylor as she brought the bowls of side dishes to the table.

The three sat down and ate dinner. Taylor told them of the conversation she had with Mrs. Hodges earlier that day.

"How did she take it?" asked Dawn.

"I don't think she believed me."

"Why would she not believe you?" asked Kenny.

"Think about it, if someone called you out of the blue and told me that you had been possibly left to die in a hospital with only one witness and that is now dead, I would think the person who called me lied or is crazy. She believes Dr. Martin and the hospital."

"That makes sense. I wonder if she called Dr. Martin?" said Dawn.

"I hope not. If she called Dr. Martin then I am sure he would tell the big boss, whoever that is. I told her that I was threatened to not look into the death of Mr. Hodges and Grandpa."

"You were threatened?" Dawn asked and looked at Taylor with a shocked look on her face. Taylor had not told anyone in her family, except Kenny.

"You should see her arm," said Kenny. Taylor looked down at her plate to avoid eye contact with her sister.

"Let me see," said Dawn. Taylor lifted up her shirtsleeve and the bruise was still a dark shade of black and blue with the fingerprints still evident. "Oh, my gosh, Taylor. Did you report this to the police?" asked Dawn as she looked at the bruises.

"No, I was told to forget everything and not to go to the police or this would be much worse."

"So, you did the exact opposite of what you were told to do?"

"Exactly," said Taylor.

"Who threatened you and where?"

"At the hospital, on the roof and a goon named Mr. Calvin, on behalf of the hospital wanted to make sure I got the message."

"Apparently that did not do any good," said Dawn looking at Taylor and then to Kenny.

"Don't look at me. I told her to report it to the police, but she did not listen to me. So good luck to you trying to change her mind," said Kenny. Taylor got up from the table and started to clear it.

Ch.44

Mr. Calvin listened to the message from Mr. Adams that night and he thought to himself, 'what now?' Mr. Calvin was in his car and just leaving for the night and he did not think that Mr. Adams would still be in his office this late, so he called him on his cell phone. He answered on the first ring.

"Mr. Calvin, I am so glad that you could call me back, but I said to come to my office."

He could tell Mr. Adams was not in a good mood.

"I am sorry, sir, I figured you would not be in your office this late," replied Mr. Calvin.

"I am still here. Now why don't you get your ass up here, now!"

"Yes, Boss. I will be there in 5 minutes," Mr.
Calvin replied quickly as the line went silent on
the other end. Mr. Calvin was not sure what he
did, but did not want to go to the lair of Mr.
Adams. Mr. Calvin had never heard him lose
his temper. He was always in control of his
emotions and never let anything bother him.
Mr. Calvin always did what he was told even if
he knew it was against his better judgment. He
did not get paid to think he got paid to do as he
was told. He got out of his large Range Rover
and walked back into the hospital. When he
approached the large office door he inhaled
deeply and then knocked.

"Enter," said Mr. Adams from the other side of
the door. Mr. Calvin opened the door and
entered the office. Mr. Calvin was a large man
and he stood in the doorway looking at the tiny
man sitting at the desk. "Close the door and
have a seat."

Mr. Calvin did as he was told. "I wanted to talk
to you in person. This situation has got out of
hand. I told you to scare her enough she would
not pursue any further into her ideas that she
had. Apparently, that was not what you did.
She did the exact opposite of what you told her."

"Boss, I don't know who you are talking about."

As Mr. Calvin said this Mr. Adams walked
around to the chair Mr. Calvin was sitting in and
bent over and wrapped his small hands around
Mr. Calvin's throat and began to choke him.

"Mrs. Bradford, you fucking idiot. Whom else would I be talking about?" Mr. Adams eyes began to shine a bright red. The past 45 years his eyes were a normal brown, but in that minute his eyes were shining a bright red.

"I, I," choked Mr. Calvin. Mr. Adams let go of his throat abruptly. Mr. Calvin coughed and cleared his throat. "I did as you asked. I thought I scared her. I threatened to kill her if she talked to anyone," Mr. Calvin was continuing to cough.

"That did not work. She called the dead man's wife. She told him that her Grandfather witnessed his death. I want you to fix this. I don't care what you have to do. Make her our patient in this hospital."

"You want me to not kill her, but injure her so she has to be sent to the hospital?"

"Exactly, do you think you can do that?"

"Sure, do you have preference on how I injure her?"

"No, just make sure she needs a hospital."

Ch.45

Taylor took Dawn to the airport early in the morning and gave her an open ended return ticket that she could use to come home again.
"Thanks Sis."
"You are welcome, I want you to come back soon," said Taylor as she kissed her sister on the cheek and gave her hug.
"Love you," said Dawn as she let go of her sister.
"Love you too. See you soon," Taylor replied as she watched Dawn go through airport security.

Taylor was sitting in her car and she thought that she had just said goodbye to her sister for the last time. She had this feeling that she would never see her again. Taylor brushed it off and started her SUV and drove to work.

Ch.46

Kenny got home early and saw the squad car drive past the house and go around the block. He was glad that Officer Grover had kept his word and he had a patrol keeping an eye on the house. Kenny was sure that Taylor had not noticed it yet. He knew if this had to continue she would notice the police car, and he would have to confess to her that he had called the police. Taylor called Kenny when she was on her way home.

"Are you home yet?" asked Taylor.

"Yea, I got home about an hour ago. Do you want to go out tonight for dinner?"

"No, I really just want to stay home with you. How does pizza sound?"

"Good. I will order it and will you pick it up?"

"Of course, I will see you soon. Love you."

"Love you too. Bye."

"Bye." Taylor hung up her cell phone and she kept driving. She had noticed that a black Range Rover was in her review mirror. She did not know who in this area would have enough money for a Range Rover. Taylor knew a lot about cars and the cost of them. It was one of her hobbies. She looked up new cars and the prices of them online and she loved the large SUV's. Her little Chevy Blazer was not expensive by any means, but it was a good car for the price. She loved Land Rovers and knew about the Range Rover. It was the luxury SUV of the two. She turned on to her short cut home, which was not paved and not many people took the road, except those that lived on the road. When she looked in her mirror the Range Rover had followed her onto the unpaved road. Taylor thought that is weird. She knew everyone on this short gravel road and no one owned a Range Rover. She continued to drive and look in the rearview mirror every few seconds. She sped up and the dust was being stirred up on the gravel road and she could no longer she the black Range Rover. Taylor turned off the dusty gravel and went on to the Hwy that took her home. She stopped at the Pizza Hut and picked up the pizza and then she continued to drive home. Out of reflex or paranoia she did not know, but she continued to look in her review mirror and did not see the Range Rover. Taylor pulled into the driveway of her house and Kenny came out of the house to help her unload her car. Taylor always had paperwork, briefcase, and her large bag she called a purse to bring in and Kenny knew she could not carry all her stuff and the pizza.

"Hey, thanks for the delivery. What do I owe ya?" asked Kenny as he walked over to her.

"A big kiss," joked Taylor.

"I don't usually pay the pizza delivery person with kisses, but I think I can bend the rules this time." Kenny reached out and cupped Taylor's face and kissed her. "I missed you today."

"I missed you to. How was your day?" asked Taylor as they walked up the steps to the house.

"It was good, but I finished up early, so I came home."

"Lucky you. I was late getting to work after I took Dawn to the airport and I had a pile of messages and I had to go to the high school to see one of my youths who got into a fight. That is why I am late." Kenny got out plates and cups for dinner and he opened the pizza box. Taylor continued to tell Kenny about her day. On my way home I could swear I was being followed."

"By who?"

"I don't know who, but they were driving a Range Rover. Newer model and black with tinted windows. I lost them on the short cut home."

"I don't like you taking the gravel road home. Especially if you thought you were being followed."

"I lost them, did you hear me?"

"What if it is someone from the hospital? That Mr. Calvin?"

"If it is I would think that they would have kept a distance from me, so I would not see them."

"Taylor, what if they were trying to scare you?"

"It did not work. If I could lose them with my little Chevy, they were not trying very hard."

"I don't like it." As Kenny said this he pulled out his cell phone and called Officer Grover. He told him about the black Range Rover.

Taylor was standing in the kitchen staring at Kenny and mouthing, "What are you doing?" Kenny hung up the cell phone and put his hands on Taylor's shoulders and looked into her eyes.

"Taylor I called Officer Grover yesterday and asked him what we should do about the hospital and Mr. Calvin. He wanted you to come into the station and fill out a report. I told him no." Taylor stopped looking at him and shook her head.

"Why would you do that? I told you I did not want to involve the police."

"I know, but I am worried and I want you to be safe. Grover put a watch on the house and a patrol car drives by at least one time per shift, to make sure everything is ok."

"You have the police watching the house?"

"Yes, I want you to be safe. You are everything to me." Kenny reached around Taylor and embraced her. Taylor pulled away and looked at him.

"Well, I guess since you have already informed the police, there is nothing I can do." Taylor picked up a piece of pizza and put in on her plate. Kenny did the same.

Ch.47

Mr. Calvin stopped his Range Rover half a block from the Bradford's. He could see the house and the cars in the driveway. All the lights in the front of the house were on. Mr. Calvin had followed Taylor home and had thought about ramming her off the road for a second, but changed his mind quickly. He loved his Range Rover and did not want to dent it. So he followed her to the pizza place and then he waited until he knew she would be home and then followed behind. He did not want her to see him pull on to her street. He was sure she saw him, but he did not worry about that. Mr. Calvin was not afraid of anyone except Mr. Adams. He had already proved to Mrs. Bradford he was much stronger than her and could over power her with one arm. He waited patiently for the lights in the house to go out.

Mr. Calvin wanted to make sure the Brad fords' were sound asleep before he made his move. Mr. Calvin had made a plan he was sure that he would not fail. He reached into his jacket pocket to feel for the Glock 9mm he carried. He got out of the Range Rover and walked to the side of the house. He was sure in such a small town; the Bradford's did not have an alarm. He was going to walk to the front door and break a small pain of glass in the door and then reach in and let himself in. When he looked back at the Range Rover he saw a police car pull up to the side and shine a light into the drivers' window. Mr. Calvin stooped low into the bushes on the side of the house. He watched as the patrolman got out of his car and kept his light shining on his Range Rover. He was talking into his radio and then walked around to the back of his pride and joy. Mr. Calvin was feeling violated. He did not like the police in general, but that was to be expected in his line of work. The police officer continued to walk around the Range Rover and look in the windows. Mr. Calvin was getting angry and wanted him to stop violating him. When the police officer reached out to the driver's door handle Mr. Calvin lost it. Mr. Calvin walked out of the bushes. "Stop right there," ordered Mr. Calvin as he reached in his jacket pocket. He pulled out his 9mm. "Turn around and put your hands up."

The Police Officer was caught off guard and not knowing what he was going to see when he turned around, he did as he was told.

"Why are you looking into my Rover?"

"I saw it sitting here with no one inside and I just wanted to take a look to make sure there was no foul play. We don't see vehicles like this just sitting on a street late at night." The Officer was trying to sound convincing he did not want to give away that he was lying. In fact he was told to look for this exact vehicle on this street and if it was found to report it to police dispatch. He had already contacted dispatch and knew Officer Grover was en route to this location.

"I don't believe you," stated Mr. Calvin. As he said that a woman's voice came over the radio the officer had on his shoulder.

"Dispatch to 148."

"That's me. I need to answer it."

"Go ahead, see what they want," order Mr. Calvin.

The officer reached his hand over to the mike on his radio. "148, go ahead dispatch."

"The Range Rover is registered to a Calvin Anderson of Sunnyville, KS. Negative 29."

"Copy that, dispatch."

"What does 'negative 29' mean?" asked Mr. Calvin.

"It means no warrants," replied the officer.

"What are you going to do with that gun?"

"I am contemplating killing you." Mr. Calvin reached into his other pocket and pulled out a gun noise suppressor. He attached it to the end of the 9mm and turned it. He walked closer to the officer and put the gun to his temple. "Now if I pull the trigger no one will hear it."

"Please, I will get into my car and pretend I never stopped and forget I ever saw you."

"Once again, I don't believe you." Mr. Calvin looked down the road and saw headlights coming. "Damn it." Mr. Calvin saw the light bar on top of the car. The patrolman saw this as an opportunity to get away from the gunman. He ducked down and rolled under the tall Range Rover, before Mr. Calvin could react to the swift movement of the patrolman, he shot his 9mm. He missed the patrolman. The gun made a quiet sound that only 2 people heard. The patrolman was on the other side of the Range Rover and drew his weapon. Mr. Calvin ran back to the cover of the bushes. He knew if he tried to get into his Rover the officer would shoot him. He did not want to die tonight. He had a mission he would complete. He would make sure Mrs. Bradford had to be taken to the hospital.

Ch.48

Officer Grover saw Officer Hill standing with his weapon drawn and taking cover behind the black Range Rover. He immediately unclipped his gun from his belt. He pulled to the side of Officer Hill's patrol car and used it as cover, so he could exit his vehicle. He slid out of the driver's seat and crouched on the ground and stepped over to Officer Hill.

"Are you being shot at?"

"Yes, I was. The owner of the vehicle has a 9mm with a suppressor. He had it pointed at my head until you came and scared him for a split second. He shot off one round as I ducked under this massive Rover."

"That's why I did not hear gunshots. Who is this guy?"

"I did not ask. He had a gun pointed at my head. I did what he said."

"Where is he now?" Officer Grover was looking left and right and behind them. He knew he would not hear a shot if they were to be shot at.

"He went in those bushes over there next to the Bradford's," replied Officer Hill. Officer Grover pulled out his cell phone and dialed Kenny Bradford's cell phone.

"Kenny, its Grover. There is a gunman outside of your house."

"What? Who is the gunman?" Kenny was now awake. Taylor woke up, when the phone rang. No one called them this late unless it was an emergency.

"We don't know who he is, but he drives a black Range Rover. I am sure it is the same Range Rover you called me about earlier this evening."

"What do you want us to do?"

"Make sure all the doors and windows are locked and then go to a room with no windows or doors and lock the door if you can, if not, barricade the door."

"Ok, call me when you know something."

"Kenny," said Officer Grover.

"Yes."

"Don't forget a gun or any weapon you may have to take it with you."

"Got it," at that Kenny grabbed Taylor's hand and pulled her out of bed and put his pants on and put his cell phone in his pocket. "Get dressed," Kenny was now in the bedroom closet and reached up to the top shelf where he kept his Grandfathers shot gun. It was always loaded. Kenny had never used it except when he went hunting.

"Kenny, what is going on?" Taylor asked, as she got dressed.

"Get your mace and make sure all the doors are locked."

"What is going on?" Taylor asked again. She had never seen Kenny act so crazy. He was scaring her.

"The Range Rover is outside our house and apparently the driver has a gun and is somewhere outside the house."

"What? Who called?"

"Grover. Now move. Meet me in the bathroom."

"Why the bathroom?"

"No windows or doors and the door locks."

"We are going to stay in here and wait for the guy with the gun to come in and try to kill us."

"He is not going to kill us, we are going to be fine. Grover is outside looking for him right now. Taylor I want you to get moving. I will check the windows and you check the doors and get your mace."

Taylor started in the back of the house and the back door was locked and she put the chain on, just to be extra safe. She went to the office to get her mace out of her purse. Kenny was running from room to room checking all the windows. It was taking him longer than usual. He came up from the bottom of the windows and then looked out before reaching up to check the locks.

Taylor went into her bedroom and got the blanket off the bed and then went into the kitchen and got out bottles of water to take in the bathroom. She did not know how long they would be barricaded in the bathroom. Kenny was in the doorway of the bathroom when she came back to the safe room that was their bathroom. Her arms were full and Kenny took the blanket and the water.

"Did you get your mace?"

"Yep right here." Taylor grabbed the small vial out of her pocket. "I forgot the front door. Be right back."

Taylor walked to the front door and noticed Kenny had drawn all the shades, so no one could see in and she could not see out. When she reached up for the chain she saw a reflection in the glass. In a matter of seconds she heard glass break and a whooshing sound and then she sprayed her mace. She was spraying wildly. She did not know what or whom she was spraying at, but it did not matter. She felt a pain in her side and a warm feeling that she had never felt before. She could not release the button on the top of the small can. She held the small can tightly in her hand. She felt hot sensation come over her and then she fell to the floor.

Ch.49

Officer Grover was coming around to the front of the Bradford's house when he saw a large man with a gun rubbing his eyes. Mr. Calvin had shot Taylor and then looked through the window he broke out to make sure she was injured and got a direct hit of the mace in his eyes.

Officer Grover walked up with his gun still drawn and yelled to the large man, "Drop your weapon and get down on the ground! Drop your weapon!" Mr. Calvin did as he was told. He was in pain and wanted to wash his eyes out. From inside the house Kenny was yelling and Officer Grover knew that he had not heard a shot and then remembered the suppressor. He kicked the gun away from the large man and kept his gun pointed at him.

"Kenny, is Taylor ok?"

"She's bleeding. She's not answering me."

"Officer Hill!" Grover yelled. "Over here, I got him." Officer Hill came from the bushes on the side of the house with his weapon drawn. He stepped up onto the front porch and pointed his gun at the head of the man lying on the ground. Mr. Calvin still had his eyes closed and was whimpering.

"Officer Hill, put him in cuffs and take him to your car. Did you hear me?"

"Yes, sir," replied Officer Hill when he awoke from a daze. He was shocked that they found him. He bent over and holstered his gun and put Mr. Calvin in handcuffs.

"I need you to call for a bus and crime scene investigators. I am going into the house Mrs. Bradford is hurt. Don't let him out of your sight."

"Got it," the officer replied. "Let's go," he told Mr. Calvin as he pulled him up on to his feet. Officer Grover reached in the broken pain of glass and unlocked the door. He stepped over the broken glass and saw Kenny holding Taylor's head in his lap and blood strewn all over the floor. Kenny's hands were colored bright red and Officer Grover saw the wound immediately. He reached down and then fell to his knees and cupped his hands over the wound on Taylor's side. "She is losing blood, but I need to see if it exited or if she still has the bullet in her."

"Bullet? She was shot? I thought she was stabbed by the broken glass."

"Kenny is she still breathing? How is her heart rate?"

Kenny put his face down to hers and could feel her breath on his face. He reached around to her arm that was lying lifeless next to her. He felt her wrist and could feel a pulse. He nodded his head up and down and Grover replied, "I am going to lift up her shirt and look at the wound and then I need you to roll her, so I can see if there is an exit wound." Kenny nodded his head again and Officer Grover kept one hand on the wound and with the other lifted her shirt up. He saw immediately the bullet had entered her right side and was not near any vital organs. He nodded and Kenny rolled her to him. Officer Grover took his hand off of the wound and lifted her shirt in the back and saw a small hole with blood coming out slowly. He had thought she would be fine if they could get her to the hospital. "Kenny, let go, so we can put her back down flat on the floor." Kenny was holding her so tight she was up on his knees and he was squeezing her and sobbing. "Kenny, she should be ok, if we could get her to a hospital. The ambulance should be here any minute. They are going to want to life line her."

"No, she is not going to the hospital. St. Anthony's did this to her and now you want me to send her there so they can finish her off. No way!"

"Kenny, it is the closest hospital."

"I don't care. She is not going to be life lined and then killed after she gets there."

"What do you want to do?"

"I don't know," Kenny started to pray he was whispering in Taylor's ear. "Dear God please let her be ok. Please let her wake up. Please, wake up Taylor."

"Kenny, hold pressure on her wound and I will be right back." Officer Grover reached over and pulled Kenny's hand to Taylor's oozing side and then got up. He went out to Officer Hill's Patrol car. Officer Hill got out of the car when he saw Grover approach.

"The bus is 10 minutes out and the backup is en route."

"I need a minute with the suspect. Did you read him his rights?"

"Yes, but I don't think he heard me. He is whining about his eyes. He says he is blind."

"Oh really. Well, let's just see if he is feeling like talking." Officer Grover got in back seat with Mr. Calvin.

"What do you want?" Asked Mr. Calvin, still rubbing his eyes.

"You shot my friend's wife and I want to know why."

"It is none of your business, pig."

"See, when you came into my town, you made it my business. Now who sent you? I know you are not smart enough to plan the deaths of patients in a hospital." Mr. Calvin looked at him with astonishment. "What, you did not think I knew about the hospital threatening Mrs. Bradford and telling her to keep quiet. Well, I do, I know everything you did. I want you to tell me about the hospital or so help me, I will make sure you get no leniency and the judge puts you in prison for the rest of your life. The judge is my father in law, so I am sure at dinner tomorrow night I could tell him exactly what kind of person you are."

"You can't do that. I have rights."

"Really, so does Mrs. Bradford, but you did not seem to care about her, now did you."

"I can't go to prison for the rest of my life. I have so much I want to do."

"Well, I guess you better start talking and fast." Mr. Calvin started to sing like a church choir. He was taking Mr. Adams and the doctors down with him. He did not want to go to prison by himself. He knew Mr. Adams would have to take the wrap for all this; he planned it and executed it all through him. Mr. Calvin did not act alone on anything he did.

"Thank you, I hope you enjoy your alone time for the next 10 to 20." Officer Grover got out of patrol car as the ambulance pulled into the driveway of the Bradford's.

Ch.50

The Paramedics had to pry Kenny off of Taylor, so they could roll her onto her back and cut her shirt up the middle. Kenny stood by and watched everything they did to her. He did not want to miss one thing they did.

Officer Grover came in a few moments later and pulled on Kenny's arm. "I need to talk to you."

"Not now."

"I have a plan."

"A plan for what?" questioned Kenny in a short direct tone.

"You don't want Taylor to go to the hospital, but if she does I am sure we will catch the man behind whole thing."

"You want me to sacrifice my wife, so you can catch a guy we don't even know and is trying to kill her." The paramedics were working on Taylor and talking amongst each other.

Kenny then heard one of the paramedics say, "We need to life line her."

"No, she is going to go in the ambulance and I am going with her. No helicopter."

"Sir, I don't know if she will make it the 45 minutes, she has lost a lot of blood and if we drive really fast maybe 30 minutes to get to the hospital."

"We are not flying her," ordered Kenny.

"Ok, let's get the IV started before we get in the bus," said the paramedic to the other and they went back to work on Taylor.

"I am going to follow the bus to the hospital and I already called my wife's cousin who is a physician in Sunnyville. He has privileges at the hospital, but is an independent doctor.   I told him Taylor's name and that she had a clean gunshot wound. He is going to meet us there and he is going to tell the ER staff that he is her family doctor and he is going to take care of her in the hospital."

"He does not work for the hospital?" questioned Kenny.

"No, he just has privileges at the hospital for his patients when they are sick."

"Does he know how to take care of her?"

"Yes, he says he has never dealt with a gunshot wound, but he says he knows what to do."

"Ok, but how is this going to get the man behind the shooting of my wife?" Asked Kenny while the paramedics were putting Taylor on the gurney.

"We're ready to go. We are taking her to St. Anthony's and who is her doctor?" interpreted one of the paramedics.

"His name is Dr. Ellison. He should be there when you arrive," replied Officer Grover.

Kenny followed behind the paramedics to the ambulance, with Officer Grover trailing.

"Kenny, it's the hospital administrator. His name is Adams. I will see you there," yelled Grover as he ran to his patrol car.

Kenny heard what Grover had said and was not sure what Officer Grover was trying to tell him. Kenny then questioned himself. Should he take his wife to St. Anthony's? He got in the back of the ambulance with one paramedic and Taylor.

Ch.51

Officer Grover was on his phone the entire drive to the hospital. He had his sirens blaring and lights going the whole way to the hospital. He was getting a sting ready at the hospital. He was a good friend of the chief of police in Sunnyville. He had told him what he only needed, to get what he wanted and needed. The plan was simple and Officer Grover wanted to make sure Kenny knew he was on his side and he was going to get the man behind this whole scandal.

Kenny was sitting next to Taylor in the ambulance holding her hand. She was cold and was lifeless. Kenny hoped she could hear him, so he continued to talk to her. He bent down to her ear and was whispering to her again. "I love you. Please don't leave me. I know you are ok with dying, but I am not ready for you to go. Please God be with her and see her back to me."

"Sir, she is stable. Her vitals are holding steady," said the paramedic.

"Good. Do you think she will be ok?"

"Yes, as long as we get some blood back in her. The hospital is ready for us. We should be there in 10 minutes."

Kenny went back to talking to Taylor, "Did you hear that? He says you will be fine."

Ch.52

When they arrived at the ER, there were a team of nurses and Dr. Ellison was waiting for them in a trauma room. Kenny was right behind the paramedics when they wheeled Taylor into the trauma room. They immediately started to look at Taylor's wound and then the Doctor ordered 2 units of blood. Kenny never took his eyes off of Taylor. He stood in the back of the room and watched. He did not want someone to slip something in Taylor's IV. "BP 88/32, pulse 54," said a nurse to the Doctor.

"Good get me a CBC, BMP. CMP and blood type and cross," said the doctor back to the nurse.

When they removed the bandage from Taylor's side, Kenny saw the wound for the first time. There was a small hole with dried blood around it and then they rolled her and Kenny saw the exit wound. It was more superficial. The bullet had entered in her right side and exited more to her side than her back. Kenny covered his face with his hands and wept. He heard the doctor talking and he was no longer listening. He felt a hand on his shoulder and he looked back he saw Grover standing there watching the doctors and nurses working on Taylor. "It will be ok, Kenny, she is going to make it."

"I know, but I did not keep her safe. I told her I would keep her safe."

"You tried and she will know that you did everything you could to keep her safe."

"I know, but I failed her, said Kenny as he rubbed his face with his blood stained hands.

"Kenny, I am going to tell you what we are going to do."

"I am staying with Taylor."

"Yes, for now I want you to, but I am going to have you leave her when she is in a room and settled."

"What? No way. I am not leaving her in this hospital. I will take her home if I have to and take care of her myself."

"Kenny, I have a plan. I told you earlier about a plan. Well, it is in motion."

"I don't understand."

"When I tell you to come and get coffee with me, I want you to come with me."

"I understand, but what are we going to do if someone tries to kill Taylor when I am not in the room?"

"Don't worry about that. I have to talk to Dr. Ellison. I will be back." Officer Grover walked up to the doctor who was now working on Taylor's wounds.

Kenny saw Grover whisper something to the Doctor and then the doctor looked back at Grover and nodded.

Officer Grover and the doctor walked back to Kenny. "Mr. Bradford, your wife is very lucky. The bullet went in her by the 3rd rib and exited out her side. She did break her rib but that will heal in time. I am now irrigating the wounds, so that she does not get an infection. I don't think we are going to have to stitch the wounds up. I would like to just put sterile dressings on them and put them on tightly and see how they do. She should not have any problems with recovery. She should be waking up soon; she has had 2 units of blood. The blood loss was her biggest problem and now that is being resolved. As soon as we get her cleaned up we are going to move her to a room and then she will stay at least overnight and maybe two nights, let's just see."

"Ok, thank you, doctor," replied Kenny.

"You're welcome."

"Can I go and see her?"

"Yes, just stay on her left side, so I can work on the right."

"Sure, thanks." Kenny walked to Taylor's side and held her hand. It was warmer than it had been in the ambulance. He bent over and kissed her hand.

"Kenny," said Taylor in a quiet voice.

"Hi," replied Kenny.

"What happened? My side is killing me."

"Almost. I thought I was going to lose you."

"I remember seeing a reflection in the glass and then glass breaking."

"You were shot, and Grover caught the guy, it was Calvin." Grover came over to the left side of Taylor with the Doctor.

"Hi, Taylor," said Grover."

"Hi," said Taylor in a small weak voice.

"This is Dr. Ellison, he is my wife's cousin."

"Hello," Taylor then realized she was at St. Anthony's. "What am I doing here? Why did you bring me to this place, Kenny? What were you thinking?"

"Taylor, Dr. Ellison does not work for St. Anthony's, he just has privileges here," said Grover.

"I need to get out of here," said Taylor.

"Mrs. Bradford, I know some of what you have been through and I assure you are safe with me. I am not paid by the hospital and I don't work for them."

"What happens when you leave? I am just supposed to lie here and hope I get to leave this hospital alive."

"Taylor, I have a plan. I am going to tell you what Calvin told me," said Grover in a calm reassuring voice.

Ch.53

Mr. Adams had a restless night. He was waiting for the call from Mr. Calvin. He was expecting him to call hours ago. He paced back and forth in his loft. He had spent a small fortune on his loft and loved it. He knew that he would pay it off in the next couple of years if business at the hospital stayed as lucrative as it had been recently. The plan of playing God had worked for him. He had built a life, which he loved. He had money, cars, a loft, membership to the country club, went on vacations, and had women at his disposal. He did not want to share his life with anyone; he loved himself too much to share it with anyone.

When his cell phone rang at 3am he jumped and was eager to hear the news on Mrs. Bradford.

"Boss, its Mr. Calvin."

"Is it done?"

"Yes, she should be at the ER now."

"Fantastic! Good job Mr. Calvin. I will see you in the morning."

"Boss, what are you going to do now?"

"Mr. Calvin, I don't want you to worry about that. Your work is done. Leave it at that."

"Yes, sir."

Mr. Adams hung up his cell phone and a large grin went across his face. He knew now Mrs. Bradford was in his hands. He could do whatever he wanted to her and no one would know how she died. Mr. Adams dialed the number to the ER.

"Dr. Foster, please," said Mr. Adams to the receptionist who answered the phone.

"Dr. Foster," he came on the line and was abrupt and tired. He had worked a double and had 4 more hours till the end of his shift.

"Dr. Foster, this is Mr. Adams."

"Well, what do I owe this call to?"

"There is a patient, who may already be there; I want you to take care of her."

"Who is it?"

"Mrs. Taylor Bradford."

"The GSW. She has her own doctor and he is taking care of her."

"Gunshot wound?"

"Yea, she was shot by an intruder and is in stable condition."

"Who is her doctor?"

"Dr. Ellison."

"He is not one of ours."

"No, but he has privileges to treat his patients in the hospital."

"Is she being released?"

"No, I believe that Dr. Ellison is admitting her."

"Good. Don't tell anyone that I called. Got it?"

"Yes, sir. Have a good night."

"You too," replied Mr. Adams. As he hung up the phone he thought how he was going to get to Mrs. Bradford. She was not in the care of one of his doctors. He knew Dr. Ellison's reputation and was not going to ask him to take of her for him. Dr. Ellison was a reputable doctor and never would agree to kill a patient.

"What to do?" said Mr. Adams as he continued to pace. "Well, I guess I can take of her myself." He felt better and went to bed and slept soundly for few hours.

Ch.54

Taylor was transferred to a room on the same floor as the ER. Kenny was with her the entire time. The morning light came through the window of her room and was a beautiful sight to her. Her gunshot wound was sore, but she felt like she had a knife in her side from the broken rib. As she lay in her bed she silently watched Kenny sleep in the chair next to the bed. He was so wonderful, she thought, 'How can I be so lucky to have a man love me so much.' Taylor knew the plan that Grover had told her just a few hours ago. She had a nurse that came in to check on her every 30 minutes, or so. She was not on the staff at the hospital either. No one would question someone in scrubs going in and out of patient rooms. At least that is what she hoped for. The nurse was actually an undercover police officer. She was not to leave the hospital until the plan had been executed. "Oh, good morning," said Kenny as he let out a yawn.

"Good morning, how did you sleep?"

"Horrible, but I am ok. Anything happen while I was out?"

"No, the 'nurse'," Taylor gestured a quotation in the air, "has been in every 30 minutes and she is close by. She put a wire under the bed so that the police can listen to everything in the room."

"I am glad that Grover had this idea, hopefully we catch the guy behind this."

"I am happy you told Grover what happened. If it was not for him we might not be here. Or at least I might not still be here." Taylor held her hand out and Kenny took it in his.

Officer Grover came in. He had went to the Sunnyville Police Department and cleaned up. He had Taylor's blood all over him, as did Kenny. Kenny had not showered. He had washed up in the sink in Taylor's room. His hands and arms were clean, but he had bloodstains on his pants and shirt still.

"How is the patient this morning?" asked Officer Grover.

"Good. You look much better," replied Kenny.

"Yea, a shower and clean clothes can do wonders," said Officer Grover looking at his neatly pressed slacks and dress shirt.

"I completely agree," said Taylor. "I would love a shower and some real clothes. I hate hospital gowns."

"You look great for someone who was shot about 10 hours ago," said Officer Grover.

"I agree with Grover, you look great."

"Thanks guys."

"Well, I came in to tell you that the plan is in motion. I can't tell you specifics, but Kenny and I are going to go and get some coffee."

"Now?" asked Kenny. He remembered that Officer Grover had told him in the ER, to go with him when he asked him to go get coffee.

"Yes, we should go get some coffee, now." Kenny got up and bent over to kiss Taylor. "I love you."

"Love you too. Don't be too long."

"I won't," said Kenny.

"We will be back soon, Taylor," said Officer Grover as he walked over to the door and waited for Kenny.

"I love you so much, Taylor."

"I know." Taylor kissed Kenny one more time and he turned and walked out with Officer Grover.

As Taylor lay in the bed and wondered what was to come next. She turned over and held her side as she did so. "Dear Lord, please keep me safe. I want to make all of this worth the pain my family has gone through. Be with me here today," said Taylor as she heard the door of her room open.

Ch.55

Taylor turned back over to see who was in her room. She grunted and let out a loud sigh as she did so. When she saw a man standing in her room, a feeling of sheer fright came over her and she felt the urge to run. She did not recognize the man, but knew he was not a good person. Often, she would have feelings about a person the first time she saw them, what kind of person they were. She did not have this feeling all the time, but today her sixth sense was completely awakened.

"Morning, Mrs. Bradford, how are you feeling?"

"Fine, who are you?" Taylor was uneasy and she knew that her voice was giving an audible tone of this.

"I am Dr. Martin," he pointed to his white coat that was over his shirt and tie, where the name, Dr. Martin, was embossed into the fabric. Taylor knew Dr. Martin from when her Grandfather was in the hospital. Dr. Martin had been Samuel's internal medicine doctor. The man before her was not Dr. Martin. She did not question the man audibly, but it was evident in her tone.

"Hello, what can I do for you?" asked Taylor.
"I am here checking on you and seeing if you need anything?"
"No, I am fine," said Taylor in a short tone.
"I heard that you have not slept since you were in the ER."
"I am not tired."
"Mrs. Bradford you need to get some rest. You will heal quicker if you rest."
"I am fine. I don't think I can sleep right now."
"I think we could give you something to help with that. How does that sound?"
"No, no thank you," Taylor replied as she started to squirm. She was trying to find a way out of this situation. She was connected to an IV and the tube was wrapped around the railing of the hospital bed.
"Mrs. Bradford," said the man claiming to be Dr. Martin in a stern voice, "I know that you have some apprehensions about the hospital, but I assure you that this won't hurt you and you could really use some sleep." The man pulled a large syringe out of the jacket pocket and it was full of a clear liquid. "This will just go into your IV and then you will fall into a deep sleep." The man was getting closer to the bed and Taylor was trying to get her IV bag down from the stand that was next to the bed and untangle her IV tubing. "Mrs. Bradford, what are you doing?" the man said in a calm voice.

Taylor looked up and saw the man's eyes had a red tint to them. "I don't want any meds to help me sleep!" Taylor said in a loud and angry voice. The sound of her voice was shaky and almost indiscernible.

The man stepped up to the side of Taylor's bed and reached out for her IV. Taylor hit him on the arm with all the force she had and grabbed her IV bag and the tubing and slid off the other side of the bed. When she hit the floor she felt the pain surge into her side. She let out a loud groan in pain. She scrambled to the underside of the hospital bed. She looked up and saw the wire that the police officer, posing as a nurse, put in her room. She yelled into the wire. "Help!"

"Who are you calling for Mrs. Bradford? No one is coming in this room. Security is outside to keep anyone from coming in. I told them that you were a delusional and combative patient and not to come in unless, I yelled for help. Not you." The man let out a laugh that was utterly evil.

Taylor realized that if anyone was coming to help her; she had to stay alive for at least a few more minutes. "Who are you really?" Taylor asked from under the bed. She began to be aware of her side feeling wet and warm again. She was lying under her bed and the floor was cold, but she had a warm, wet feeling on her side. She looked down and saw blood coming from her hospital gown. She glanced back up and saw the man's face. He had stooped down to see under the bed.

"Mrs. Bradford, I am the hospital. I am the beginning and the end of life here. Until you came along, no one ever questioned my authority."

"You are the one who sent Mr. Calvin after me?" Taylor asked as she squirmed to the back of the underside of the bed.

"You are finally showing your intelligence, Mrs. Bradford. I thought you knew as soon as I came in the room and you looked at me."

"I did. I know who you weren't. I know Dr. Martin and you are not him."

"Very good, Mrs. Bradford, a miscalculation on my part. I just grabbed a jacket out of the doctors' lounge and until I put it on before I entered your room, I did not know whose jacket I had grabbed. Let me properly introduce myself, I am Mr. Jack Adams, the hospital administrator, or you can call me the God of St. Anthony's." Mr. Adams pulled off the white coat and reached under the bed with one hand. In the other he still had the large syringe of liquid.

"Get away from me!" yelled Taylor. She flailed her legs and held her side that was now spewing blood onto her hands and her hospital gown.

"Why are you making this so difficult?" asked Mr. Adams as he grabbed a hold of her foot and pulled.

Taylor felt the tug on her foot and she let go of her side and with both hands grabbed at the bars on the underside of the bed. She held on as Mr. Adams pulled at her foot with one hand. Taylor let out a loud groan, "Arrga!"

"Let go and all this will be over," said Mr. Adams, as he continued to pull on Taylor's bare foot. "You are the most difficult patient I have ever had to kill," said Mr. Adams impatiently. "Most of the patients I have to get rid of are clinging to life anyway, and don't put up a fight."

Taylor heard a commotion in the hallway and she knew that she could not hold on for even a second longer. She felt the cold steel slip from her fingertips and then the cold floor underneath her head. She knew she was being slid out from under the bed and then she saw blackness.

Ch.56

Kenny and Officer Grover were arguing with the two security guards outside Taylor's room.

"Move out of the way!" yelled Kenny.

"Sir, we are not supposed to leave our post; we cannot let you in," said one of the guards.

"This is a police matter, now move!" ordered Officer Grover, as he pulled out his police badge.

"I am sorry officer, but you are not allowed into this room. We were ordered not to let anyone in or out," said the other guard, as he stretched his arms out across the hospital room door.

Kenny was now losing his patients. He knew Taylor was just on the other side of the door and the only thing between him and her were 2 large men. Kenny walked up to one and hit him in the stomach and pulled him down by the collar and threw him on to the floor.

Officer Grover saw this and reached up and hit the other guard in the face and then kneed him in the groin. Kenny opened the door to the hospital room and Officer Grover followed behind with his gun drawn.

Kenny saw a man on the floor with Taylor lying over his legs and her IV in his hands. He was pushing the end of a large syringe with half it already in her IV tube.

"Drop the syringe and put your hands up!" order Officer Grover, while pointing his gun at the man's back. Mr. Adams did what he was told and stood up. Taylor fell lifeless to the floor.

"You are too late," said Mr. Adams with grin. Kenny ran to her and fell to the floor next to her and yanked her IV out of her arm. He was not sure what the man had put in her IV, but knew he did not want it in her. The hole in Taylor's hand, let by the IV, bled onto Kenny's already blood stained jeans. He lifted her head, "Help, I need some help in here!"

A Nurse and a Doctor came rushing in the room and at first were stunned to see Mr. Adams at gunpoint being held against the wall of the hospital room.

"Here, down here," ordered Kenny.

The nurse came up and pushed Kenny to the side and reached down and felt for a pulse.

"She's got a pulse, weak and thready."

"Lets get her up to the bed," said the young doctor who came in the room. "Why is her IV pulled out?"

"I pulled it out. That man was putting this in her arm." Kenny reached down and picked up the large syringe that was still in her IV.

"What is in it?" Questioned the doctor as he began to lift Taylor's eyelids to look at her eyes and then he said, "We need O2."

"Yes, doctor," said the nurse.

Officer Grover turned Mr. Adams around and looked into his eyes. "What's in the syringe, asshole?"

Mr. Adams did not respond; he smiled. The smile was eerie and made Kenny even angrier. He walked over and lifted the syringe up to Mr. Adams face. "What is in this syringe?"

Mr. Adams did not respond again. Kenny repeated his question, "Did you hear me? I said, what is in the syringe?"

Then his mouth parted slightly and he spoke, "It's a simple mixture of ketamine and morphine," said Mr. Adams with a smile still on his face.

Kenny did not know what ketamine was, but he knew what morphine was and the syringe that Mr. Adams had used was a 30cc syringe and that much morphine would put a horse to sleep for hours.

The young doctor working on Taylor had a look of terror on his face. He looked up from the lifeless Taylor that laid before him, at the nurse rushing back into the room. The Nurse brought back an O2 mask and immediately put it on Taylor's face.

"How much is left in the syringe?" asked the doctor.

Kenny looked down and replied, "15, the plunger is at 15."

The nurse looked down at Taylor's IV tubing and saw that it was full of the clear liquid and it was spilling onto the floor. "Doctor, there is still some in the IV and on the floor."

"Well, let's hope he did not get all 15ml in her."

"What will happen if he did?" asked Kenny.

Mr. Adams spoke up again, "She will have hypertension, respiratory failure, apnea, then, hypotension, bradycardia, cardiac arrhythmias, and then cardiac failure." He still had a smile on his face and Kenny wanted to beat the smile off of his face. Before he had a chance Officer Grover turned Mr. Adams back to the wall and pushed him up against it.

"That will be enough out of you," said Officer Grover.

"He is right, sir, she will go into respiratory failure if he did put all 15ml in her."

The nurse was franticly putting a new IV in Taylor and the doctor was working on stopping the bleeding from her side. "Did someone page Dr. Ellison?"

"Yes, doctor I did when I went out to get the nonrebreather mask."

"Good we might need to put her on a vent as soon as he gets here."

"A vent?" asked Kenny. "She's going to need a ventilator?"

"She might need it for about the first 24 hours. It would be to prevent her lungs from failing. Nurse I need a CBC, and a chemical panel for morphine and ketamine, stat."

"Yes, doctor."

Ch.57

Officer Grover had taken Mr. Adams out of the room in hand cuffs. He wanted to walk him out of the hospital in handcuffs, so that every doctor and nurse could see him in shackles. Officer Grover did not want anyone else to transport Mr. Adams.   He did not know how far his power reached, but wanted to make sure Mr. Adams was put into a cell and locked up. In the patrol car Officer Grover made calls to the prosecuting attorney and the Judge of Sunnyville.

In the back seat Mr. Adams still was smiling. He was sure that he would get out of this. The only person who knew the truth was now in a comatose state and would hopefully die in the next 24 hours. Officer Grover saw the man still smiling in his back seat. He looked into the rearview mirror, "I see you have that shit eating smile still on your face."

"Why, should I not?"

"Since you are going to be in prison for the rest of your life, I would think that you would stop smiling."

"Prison?" Mr. Adams let out a laugh, "I am going to spend about 2 hours at the fine Sunnyville Police Department and then go back to work."

"Oh really, why do you think I arrested you?"

"For practicing medicine, without a license."

"No, I am arresting you for murder of countless patients, and for the attempted murder of Taylor Bradford."

"You have no proof."

"I have you confessing on tape and also, the struggle with Mrs. Bradford on tape as well."

"How do you have that?"

"The wire was under the hospital bed in Taylor's room. I heard it all in a van outside the hospital. Oh, yes I heard it all and soon a jury will hear it all. Not to mention we have a little bird already in jail singing for his life," laughed Officer Grover.

"What are you talking about?' Mr. Adams was now angry and he was no longer smiling.

"A Mr. Calvin, was arrested last night at the Bradford's residents."

"No, that is not possible."

"Why, because he called you last night? Well, we persuaded him to call you, and you did exactly what I thought you would do."

"I can not believe this. No, I don't believe any of this," said Mr. Adams as he began to shake his head.

"You can choose not to believe it, but it is so true and I cannot wait for you to rot in prison."

Officer Grover reached into his jacket pocket and pulled out the tape from the recorder. He had reached under Taylor's bed before he left and pulled the tape out.

"You see this tape; it is going to seal your fate." Officer Grover waved it front of the cage separating him from Mr. Adams.

Mr. Adams was livid. He kicked at the cage in front of him.

Ch.58

Kenny was sitting in a chair next to Taylor's bed. He had not been able to leave her for even a second. He had blood stained jeans, shirt, arms, and hands. He called Taylor's parents and they were on their way to the hospital. They were angry with Kenny for not calling them when Taylor was shot. He tried to explain that there was a plan to catch the man who was behind the shooting and if he had called them they would have gotten in the way.

"So, you wait until our daughter is on a ventilator and fighting for her life, before calling us. We could have talked to her earlier and now we can't," scolded Olivia.

Kenny just took the scolding. He knew that Olivia would not normally talk to him like that and he did not want to say anything that he would regret later.

He sat in the darkness of the room with only the lights on the ventilator and the vital sign monitor lighting the room. The sound of the machine breathing for Taylor was ominous. Kenny sat and remembered Taylor talking about Samuel and when he was on a ventilator, how the sound made her crazy. Kenny now understood. The whooshing and the deflating sound of the machine was almost enough to drive a sane person insane.

Taylor would have to be on the ventilator for at least the first 24 hours and then if she woke up they would take her off of it. Kenny was hoping that she would wake up soon. She had been given a new IV and 2 more units of blood. She had bled out of her gunshot wound again and needed to be replenished. Kenny thought that she would wake up once she got the refill of blood, but she did not.

Dr. Ellison came in and turned on the light above Taylor's bed. Kenny immediately opened and then closed his eyes at the brightness of the light.

"Sorry, Kenny, I need to check on her."

"That's ok, doc, I need to wake up anyway. Taylor's parents will be here soon," said Kenny while rubbing the sleep out of his eyes.

"Good, there is not much that they can do or you can do for her. You need to get some rest and change your clothes."

Kenny looked down and realized that he was a mess. "Yea, I need a lot of things, but I am not leaving her."

"How about I get you some scrubs and when Taylor's parents get here, you go into that bathroom and shower and change your clothes."

"Thanks doc. That sounds great."

"Good, I am glad that's settled. Now let's look over our patient." Dr. Ellison took his stethoscope out and listened to Taylor's heart. Then he took out his penlight and opened her eyes.

Kenny thought about the last time he saw her beautiful eyes open and telling her that he loved her, when he left her in that hospital room, as bait. Tears fell from his eyes and he wiped them away as soon as they hit his cheeks.

"She should wake up soon, Kenny. I am expecting her to have a full recovery. I am only concerned about the next 18 hours. The most important thing now is keeping her breathing."

"I know, I was just thinking about the last time her eyes were open."

The door of the room opened Olivia and Jerry Kingsley came charging in. "Kenny, how is she?" asked Jerry.

"She is unchanged since I called you."

"Hello, I am Dr. Ellison. I have been taking care of your daughter since she came into the ER last night," said Dr. Ellison to Taylor's parents.

"Where were you when someone tried to kill her today?" said Olivia in an angry voice.

"Olivia!" Yelled Jerry.

"That's ok, sir, I understand," said Dr. Ellison. "I was not here, as instructed by the police and I am truly sorry."

Olivia began to cry and Jerry took her in his arms. Kenny stood up and walked over to them to hug them. "Kenny, you are a mess," said Olivia while wiping her tears.

"I know, I was waiting for you to get here to stay with Taylor while I get cleaned up."

"At that note I will go get you some scrubs," said Dr. Ellison and he turned and left the room.

"Is she going to wake up?" asked Olivia as she walked over and picked up Taylor's hand.

"Yes, Dr. Ellison said that she should wake up, but the ventilator has to stay on her for at least 24 hours, if she doesn't wake up first."

"What was she thinking? Why would she do this?" Asked Olivia.

"She wanted to tell Mrs. Hodges how her husband really died."

"Who is Mrs. Hodges?" asked Jerry.

Kenny forgot that Taylor had not told anyone what she was doing. "Samuel told Taylor about a man he saw die in this hospital and he was scared that he would be killed for witnessing it." Kenny continued to tell Taylor's parents about the phone calls, the threat, the records, Dr. Killsmen, the shooting, and the plan to catch the hospital administrator.

"I can't believe she did all of this and not tell us. We are her parents," said Olivia.

"She did not tell anyone, except me. I told Officer Grover about the whole thing after she was threatened and I am glad I did."

Dr. Ellison came in and gave Kenny a set of scrubs. "Thank you, doc," said Kenny as he took the top and bottom set of scrubs. "Will you two please, stay with Taylor while I get cleaned up?"

"Of course, Kenny," said Jerry.

"Don't let any doctors come in and do anything to her. Understand?" ordered Kenny as he got up to go to the bathroom.

"I thought the hospital administrator was in jail?" asked Jerry.

"He is, but he has doctors in the hospital that work for him and I don't know how loyal they are."

"Ok, Kenny," replied Olivia. "Now go get cleaned up, before she wakes up."

Kenny turned back around and walked over to the side of Taylor's bed. He bent over and whispered in her ear and then kissed her cheek. Taylor did not respond. She continued to lay in a deep sleep.

Ch.59

The following morning Kenny was awoke by Officer Grover.

"You look like shit."

"Thanks, I feel like it," replied Kenny.

"I have great news. Mr. Jack Adams has been charged and held without bond on 1 count of attempted murder and pending indictment on several murder charges of countless patients."

"Fantastic."

"It gets better. Mr. Calvin is going to be a witness for the prosecution and he is pointing fingers at some of the doctors and they are getting picked up as we speak. The FBI is involved now and the Catholic Church is denying all allegations or connection to this conspiracy."

"Of course they are."

"Mr. Calvin has said that at least 2 of the priests in the hospital are also involved. The catholic church is also denying that."

"Are the 2 priests going to be questioned as well?"

"I am sure the FBI will do that, but there is a lot of red tape when it comes to questioning men of the cloth."

"I guess there would be."

"Mr. Calvin, also, had information on Samuel. He said that Mr. Jack Adams ordered the doctors not to treat Samuel for an infection that he developed after he had the lung biopsy. He claims that after Samuel witnessed Mr. Carl Hodge's death Mr. Adams did not want any lose ends."

"Samuel was considered a lose end?" asked Kenny as he shook his head in disbelief, that someone could be so cruel to another human being.

"Yea, he thought that Samuel would have eventually talked and then there would have been a lawsuit filed against the hospital by the relatives of Carl Hodges."

"That is awful, but Taylor will be ecstatic."

"How is she?" asked Officer Grover.

"She's the same. She has not woken up yet. Dr. Ellison thinks she will wake up soon."

"How much longer is she going to be on that thing?"

"The ventilator?"

"Yea."

"Well, hopefully she will be taken off of it tonight, if she does not wake up before then."

"Good. I can't wait to tell her the news."

"She will be so happy," said Kenny.

When he looked up at her face he saw her eyes twitching. He stood up and leaned over her. Her eyes continued to twitch and then they opened and closed again.

"Go and get a nurse or Dr. Ellison if he is here." Officer Grover ran out of the room and into the hallway.

"Taylor wake up," said Kenny as he took her head into his hands.

Her eyes twitched again and Kenny took a hold of her shoulders. "Taylor, wake up, please. I need you."

Taylor's eyes twitched again and then they opened.

"Taylor," Kenny said as his eyes filled with tears. He bent over and kissed her forehead.

Dr. Ellison entered the room with Office Grover following.

"She's awake," said Kenny excitedly.

Dr. Ellison looked into Taylor's eyes. "Taylor can you hear me? Blink once for yes."

Taylor did as instructed and blinked once.

"Good. There is a tube in your throat connected to a ventilator. It is there to help you breath. Do you understand?" explained Dr. Ellison.

Taylor blinked once. Taylor tried to remember the last thing that happened before she lost consciousness. She remembered the underside of the hospital bed and being pulled on, by her foot. She then remembered Mr. Adams; he was trying to kill her. She tried to sit up and then fell back down on to the bed.

"Don't try to move. You are going to have some dizziness and I don't want you pass out," said Dr. Ellison.

"Can you take the vent off now?" asked Kenny with anticipation.

"I suppose in the next hour if she stays awake and her vitals are stable, we can. Taylor you need to stay awake and then we will take the tube out of your throat."

Taylor blinked once.

"I will be back in an hour. Make sure she does not fall back asleep," said Dr. Ellison.

Ch.60

Kenny and Officer Grover told Taylor all about
what had happened while she was unconscious.
She could not respond to them, but was elated.
She thought how great it was that all of this was
not for nothing. Taylor looked at Kenny and
could not figure out why he was wearing scrubs.
She reached up and grabbed his scrub top.
"Like the new duds?"
Taylor shook her head no.
"Well I did not bring a change of clothes with
me to the hospital and Dr. Ellison found these
for me. My jeans and my shirt, I think, are
beyond washing."
Taylor blinked at him. She thought how much
she loved him and could not wait to get this tube
out of her throat to tell him.

Olivia and Jerry came back up to the hospital and when they entered the room they both were elated that Taylor had woken up. "We are so glad that you decided to wake up, sleeping beauty," said Jerry.

Taylor blinked and then she tried to smile. "The blink means she understands you," said Kenny.

"How much longer is she going to have to be on the ventilator?" asked Olivia.

"No much longer. Dr. Ellison is going to come back anytime and check on her and since she has stayed awake they should take the tube out."

Ch.61

Kenny, Olivia, Jerry, and Officer Grover waited outside Taylor's room. Dr. Ellison did not want the family in the room when they took the tube out of Taylor. "It is not a very nice procedure and we will let you back in once we are done," said Dr. Ellison as he ushered the family outside. Kenny did not want to leave her again. He thought about the last time he left her in that room and when he fought his way back to her, she almost died.

"How much longer is this going to take?" Asked Olivia impatiently.

"Hopefully not much longer," replied Kenny.

As he said this, the door opened and Dr. Ellison came out.

"She is stable and her oxygen level is at 98% on room air. She won't be able to talk, but she can whisper. I encourage you to all offer her many ice chips and then give her water, as she wants. It will help soothe her throat and her vocal cords."

"Thank you, doctor," said Olivia.

Kenny shook Dr. Ellison's hand and then walked directly into the room.

"Let's give him a few minutes," said Jerry.

When Kenny saw her sitting upright with her eyes open he almost forgot everything that she had been through and wanted to scoop her up and take her home. "How are you feeling?" asked Kenny.

"Ok, my throat hurts," whispered Taylor.

"I am so happy that you are going to be ok."

"Dr. Ellison said that I would be ok. There is something that I want to tell you, but I don't know if this is the right time," Taylor said softly. Kenny sat down on the side of the bed and reached over and picked up Taylor's hand. "You can tell me anything."

Taylor looked into Kenny's eyes and softly said, "Kenny, I am pregnant."

"What?" Kenny asked with a look of shock on his face.

"Dr. Ellison told me when you all were out waiting for the tube to be taken out. He said that I should not keep my hopes up. He says that everything I have been through would be hard on any pregnancy, especially one in the first trimester."

Kenny did not know what to say. He thought about telling her everything would be ok, but he was not sure. "How far along are you?"

"Maybe 6 weeks. I have not been keeping track."

"What can we do?" asked Kenny.

"Nothing, just wait and see if the baby holds on. He says that there's an OB doctor he recommends and that I should get in to see her right away, given the circumstances."

Kenny was shocked and was not sure he should be happy yet. He always knew that Taylor and he would have children, but he did not want to get excited and then have it all taken away.

"Taylor, I think we should wait to tell anyone."

"I agree. I don't want to get my parents hopes up and then have a miscarriage."

"Maybe the baby is stronger than we think."

"Hopefully," Taylor struggled to get the words out.

"You should not try to talk, so much."

"Yea, save some of your voice for us," said Jerry as he and Olivia entered.

"I am so glad that you are ok," said Olivia.

"Me too," replied Taylor softly.

"Can I come in?" asked Officer Grover as he cracked the door open and looked in.

Taylor waved her hand in the air.

"Of course, our family owes you so much," said Jerry.

"No, Taylor here took the worst of it. I was just in the right place at the right time."

"No, you were the answer to my prayers," whispered Taylor.

"What? No," said Officer Grover as his cheeks turned a reddish pink color.

"I asked the lord to help me through this whole mess and he used Kenny to make sure the right person was involved who could help me. That's you," Taylor looked up at Officer Grover, "Thank you."

"You my dear are so very welcome. Besides, I don't mind being used for the Lord's work."

"Me neither," said Kenny and everyone laughed.

Ch.62

4 months later

"Did you see the paper this morning?" asked Kenny.

"Yep, I am so glad all of this is over," replied Taylor.

"I doubt it is, there is still appeals and I am sure Jack Adams won't go quietly to prison for life without taking as many as he can down with him."

"I know, but I dreamt about him last night. He was in a small cell and he was on his knees on cold, gray cement. There were chains being thrown around him. I could not see who was putting the chains around him, but I could see hundreds of people standing around him and they were watching intently, as the chains got tighter and the chains got to be so heavy that he fell to the cement floor."

"Taylor, your dreams are so messed up. I dream about pie and new cars; you dream about people dying and facing judgment."

"I hope he realizes what he is going to face in the afterlife."

"You aren't going on another mission, are you?" questioned Kenny.

"No, I think that I will leave this one up to God," replied Taylor.

"Good. We are almost there."

Taylor looked up and saw the large rock bluff ahead of her. It had been 6 months since she had been able to get back out on the lake. She wanted to go back to where it all began and to tell Samuel everything that had happened. She knew she could talk to him at any time, but she felt closer to him out on the lake in his boat, than anywhere in the world.

"Are you going to tell him, he is going to be a Great Grandfather?" asked Kenny.

"I am sure he already knows," said Taylor as she looked down at her large stomach and rubbed her hand across it.